Lord Archer Catches a Contessa

Windermeres in Love Series
Book Two

Sofie Darling

ARE YOU SIGNED UP FOR DRAGONBLADE'S BLOG?

You'll get the latest news and information on exclusive giveaways, exclusive excerpts, coming releases, sales, free books, cover reveals and more.

Check out our complete list of authors, too!

No spam, no junk. That's a promise!

Sign Up Here

www.dragonbladepublishing.com

Dearest Reader;

Thank you for your support of a small press. At Dragonblade Publishing, we strive to bring you the highest quality Historical Romance from some of the best authors in the business. Without your support, there is no 'us', so we sincerely hope you adore these stories and find some new favorite authors along the way.

Happy Reading!

CEO, Dragonblade Publishing

Additional Dragonblade books by Author Sofie Darling

Windermeres in Love Series
Lady Amelia Takes a Lover (Book 1)
Lord Archer Catches a Contessa (Book 2)

Dedication

To Eric, always.

Chapter One

London
June 1821

ARCHIE STEPPED INSIDE the Five Graces theater, holding a mug of beer in each hand, and felt immediately at home.

Not that he should.

He was a lord, after all. Lord Daniel Windermere, Viscount Archer, in fact.

And the Five Graces?

Well, it was a theater of "low" entertainment. A place where London accents ranged too broadly for the narrow confines of Mayfair drawing rooms. A place where bodies jammed up against each other without anyone giving such proximity a second thought. A place that, frankly, stank.

A place that Archie loved down to the marrow of his noble bones.

"Archie!" came a shout.

Above the fray, he found his best friend in the world, Lord Rory Macbeth, Viscount Kilmuir—his world overflowed with titled gentlemen—waving at him from their usual spot—fifth row, dead center. Archie was adamant on that point. Whoever arrived first secured that pair of seats. From them, one could sink into the performance and, most importantly, the music.

His eye flicked toward the edge of the stage. Half hidden behind musty brown velvet curtains sat the piano, emitting the jangly tunes that would serve as the musical accompaniment tonight. Sitting at the keyboard was George Fry, his nimble fingers flying across the keys, only missing a note here and there. The man was quite proficient for never having had a proper piano lesson in his life.

Archie, on the other hand, had plowed through years and years of lessons. Sure, he'd groused and complained like any child, but he and his instructor had known the truth.

That Archie's very soul was contained in those keys.

He entered the fifth row of seats, an apologetic smile on his mouth, one meant to charm as he jostled through, avoiding the knees of those already seated and stepping over entire laps when necessary, all without spilling a single, solitary drop of beer.

Still, his smile got him through. His was the sort of smile that charmed both women and men—women into his bed and men into friendship.

"Rory, old chap," he called out.

"You're late. I thought you were going to miss tonight." Rory accepted the mug of beer into his massive bear paw of a hand. He was a great lumbering fellow by anyone's measure. With his head of auburn hair and towering height, he lacked English elegance and refinement, which was just as well, given he was Scottish. Since the day they'd met at Eton, Archie and Rory had been fast friends.

"Not a chance," said Archie, holding up his mug in a silent toast before knocking back a large swallow.

"What do you know about tonight's entertainments?" asked Rory, swiping foam off his top lip.

"It'll include a scene from Shakespeare, I believe," said Archie.

Rory groaned. "Not bloody Shakespeare." He took another great swallow of drink. With the surname Macbeth, Rory had suffered through enough Shakespeare jokes to last three lifetimes, half of them told by Archie. "I was hoping they'd got that lass on the swing back."

Archie snorted. "Don't we all."

Rory's bright blue eyes lit up in a wistful smile. "She was truly quite skilled with the way she could flip up and down and around that swing. It never failed to impress."

"Or leave much to the imagination," said Archie, wry.

"Well," said Rory, his grin turned boyishly roguish, "two things can be true at once."

The stage lights flickered three times, informing the audience that the night's entertainment was set to begin.

Archie settled back into his seat, careful not to give the impression that he was wholly, utterly, perhaps desperately, invested. For him, music was no idle or trifling thing, even in a place like the Five Graces, whose stage offered up all manner of entertainments on any given night. Singers... Musicians... Acrobats... Magicians... He'd once seen a bear with a white ruff around his neck dance across this stage.

But it was the music that drew him in Thursday after Thursday. To be sure, it wasn't refined or remotely elegant, but it pulsed with a raw energy one didn't find in the tame drawing rooms of the *ton*.

This place held the promise of inspiration. Something that had been in short supply since he'd returned from Italy with his sisters last year. For him, these Thursday night entertainments were serious business, even if to all the world he looked like nothing more than a carefree aristocrat out for a lark—a look that was his particular specialty.

The Lord Archer the *ton* knew was always up for a jape with his ever-present, devil-may-care smile.

Only he knew the truth of his passions.

Passion.

Singular.

Music.

It was everything to him.

Perhaps his sisters understood a bit of it, for it was known he was quite proficient at the piano. But he desired to be more than merely proficient, good, or even great. For here was the thing: his music, it obsessed him.

And when he watched a musician on stage—like George Fry up there now—inspiration sparked within him, and something else, too. *Envy.* Those men and women performing tonight were professional musicians, making a living from their skill.

He wasn't.

He was simply a viscount who would someday be an earl.

In truth, he'd been at odds and ends since returning from Italy. It was the blasted composition he'd been working on for months. He hadn't been able to get anywhere with it since setting foot on English soil. It was as if the muse had entirely abandoned him.

Apparently, his muse was Italian.

George Fry did something interesting with a minor key, and it sparked a little something within Archie. Perhaps his muse wasn't Italian at all, but rather a Cockney gent from the East End.

The first performer was a man with a monkey. The act centered around the monkey being more refined than the handler, much to the delight of the crowd. Next came the Shakespeare. Although it was a scene from a comedy, Rory groaned and shut his eyes, snatching a quick nap. Then out sauntered a magician with a flamboyant flourish of his cape, his assistant trailing behind.

Archie sat forward in his seat. He attempted to pay attention to the magic tricks, but his eye kept straying toward the assistant. The woman was quite fetching with sable brown hair that hung loose to the small of her back and luminous brown eyes and full, luscious lips the color of rubies.

That mouth… It was made for sin.

He should elbow Rory, for he knew his friend would want to catch an eyeful of her, but Archie couldn't.

He wanted her for himself.

Whistles and catcalls shot through the haze of desire that had begun building inside him. Once he paid attention to the actual performance, he saw what was obvious to everyone in the theater.

For all her beauty, the woman was a terrible magician's assistant.

She gave away one trick after another before the magician could complete them. Further, the more purple-faced and frustrated the magician grew, the more flustered and clumsy the assistant became, worsening the cycle to the point of farce.

Yet Archie couldn't laugh along with his fellow theatergoers. Usually, he found this crowd invigorating in its democratic response to performance. If it was great, they cheered loudly. If it was terrible, they booed just as loudly. Tonight…

It felt like bullying.

Tonight, he felt the distinct urge to punch someone in the nose.

Over what?

Over a performer who had no business being on the stage?

Perhaps it was kinder this way. Perhaps the woman would realize the stage was no place for her and find another form of employment. Perhaps the crowd was doing her a favor.

Within minutes, thankfully, the magician and his beautiful, but hapless, assistant were ushered off stage by the *compère*. Rory startled awake, his blue eyes wide and unfocused. "What did I miss?"

"The magic act."

"Oh, blast, why didn't you wake me? The magicians are my favorite. Did he pull a rabbit out of a hat?"

"He did not."

What the magician had done was pull a fair amount of lint from his hat, and the rabbit had hopped across the stage as if looking for his lost warren. Judging by the thunderous expression on the magician's face, this, too, had been the fault of the assistant.

How had such a thoroughly untalented woman found her way onto the stage? The Five Graces might not have been the height of sophistication, but it was known for both its variety of performers and the quality of those performers.

He snorted.

It was her beauty, of course.

Rory slung back the remainder of his beer and burped into his hand. "Want another?"

"Funny you should ask," said Archie, holding up his empty mug.

While Rory was gone, another two quick acts followed the magician. A scruffy, little dog who could perform all manner of tricks, including dancing on his hind legs, and a mime, who had the crowd transfixed by his inability to climb out of an invisible box.

Rory had just returned when the *compère* announced the next act. "It is my pleasure to introduce an opera singer making her stage debut tonight."

Beside Archie, Rory groaned. "There are any number of drawing rooms in Mayfair where I could listen to a young lady caterwaul her way through Mozart, if that's what I wanted."

"A most beauteous young lady come all the way to our shores from enchanting Italy," continued the *compère*, with a dramatic swish of his cape. *"La Contessa!"*

Into the quiet following the *compère*'s announcement stepped a woman, halting and unsure. She was dressed like a ghost from the last century with her tall white powdered wig, beauty mark placed on a high cheekbone, and wide pannier skirt. The costume was utterly ridiculous, which made it perfect for the Five Graces.

What wasn't perfect?

Archie recognized the woman as the magician's assistant.

Rory sat forward. "Now what do we have here?"

"She's a stunner," said Archie. Might as well get the obvious out of the way.

"Think she's a real contessa?"

"Doubtful," said Archie, dry.

Italian, he could allow with her luminous brown eyes and olive complexion.

But a contessa?

Not a chance.

Contessas didn't sing for this crowd.

Rory shrugged. "Who would care anyway?"

An undeniable fact.

Hands clasped so tightly her knuckles shone white, she cleared her throat, thereby silencing half the crowd. She waited thirty seconds more, subtly shifting from foot to foot, clearly hoping the other half would follow the lead of their fellows. They didn't.

Archie felt his hands clenching in his lap as he grew unaccountably angry. This was nothing short of a crime. To drag this woman on stage and offer her up as ridicule for the entertainment of the public...

She cleared her throat and opened her mouth, and a sound poured forth, filling the air, as voice after voice fell away and all that was left was hers, the entirety of the room suddenly enraptured by her. Archie couldn't believe his ears, for what he was hearing was a pure high mezzosoprano without flaw—nothing less than the voice of an angel. It left him no choice but to sit back in his seat and let her voice flow over him, sink into him, and fill his soul with nourishment he hadn't been aware he'd been craving all his life until this very moment.

She stepped forward, her voice strengthening in confidence. No longer was she a hapless magician's assistant, but a woman in control—of herself, of this room. Her gaze roved across the crowd as she sang Handel's *"Lascia ch'io pianga"* aria. It was delicate and mournful and pure magnificence. Then her gaze landed on his, and the breath froze in Archie's chest.

Eyes locked, the world simply fell away—only him and her, as if he could feel each individual cell of blood flowing through his veins.

Her gaze shifted, and the connection broke, like that.

The aria ended, and she stood before the audience, eyes shining, cheeks glowing, chest heaving. The collective breath held under the spell she'd woven.

Archie felt winded...invigorated...*inspired*.

He needed more of it.

He needed more of *her*.

He shot to his feet, clapping like a maniac. Half a second later the room followed on a roar. Everyone understood what they'd witnessed. Talent supreme... *Magic*.

Archie wanted more.

He glanced over at Rory, who was as awestruck as the rest of the room. "I'll see you on the morrow for our morning ride?"

A crease formed between Rory's eyebrows. "You're hanging up your hatchet already?"

Not exactly, but he'd no intention of explaining to his friend the urges pulling at him. If he told Rory he was heading backstage to meet the singer, Rory would get all nudge-nudge winky-winky and possibly waggle his eyebrows.

And this wasn't *that*.

Well, maybe a little. The woman was attractive in the earthy, voluptuous way that, well, Archie rather liked.

But he *needed* to be in her presence, for other reasons. Reasons having to do with the muse now flowing through him.

He gave Rory a firm nod of farewell and began pushing through the crowd that had begun booing the *compère*. The audience wanted more of *her*, and preferably with fewer clothes. *Philistines*.

Yet...

Why was she singing at the Five Graces? Her technique and stage sense weren't yet perfected, but she was young and those skills would come with proper guidance.

Didn't she understand her worth?

While the crowd remained mostly distracted by the contortionist who had taken to the stage, Archie slipped behind the dusty brown curtain, and found himself in the midst of another sort of chaos—tetchy performers hying to and fro as they readied themselves. Here sat a clown in silent contemplation. There a dancer shouting for a glass of water while applying a thick coating of kohl to her eyebrows.

"La Contessa?" Archie asked a woman who was combing the fur of the monkey he'd seen take the stage earlier.

The woman silently pointed her comb in the direction of a short, dark corridor, and Archie followed it to a room that appeared to be empty at first glance. Except it wasn't empty. There, behind a screen in the corner, flickered orange candlelight.

He strode over and peered around the wooden frame. Back to him, she sat before a dressing table. Wig off, she was half undressed, down to chemise, corset, and drawers. He knew from other backstage visits that performers weren't too fussy about their state of dress—or undress.

"Contessa?" he spoke into the silence.

Luminous brown eyes shifted and met his in the mirror, and he experienced that jolt again. As if a vise had tightened in his chest.

"*Buona sera,*" he said, choosing to greet her in Italian.

She simply nodded and resumed wiping stage makeup off her face. He sensed he'd been dismissed.

He'd once heard his smile described as pure sunshine. Yet this woman remained utterly, fixedly unmoved. Not charmed in the least.

His intrigue only grew.

He was always intrigued by the ones who didn't give him the time of day.

When he made no movement to leave, her gaze met his again in the mirror. "Well?" she asked, the single word more demand than question.

Archie knew a few truths at once. The woman wasn't Italian, and certainly no contessa. But she wasn't from London, either. With that one *well*, he had her down as a country lass.

What was a lass from the country named La Contessa doing singing German opera in Southwark?

"*Well*, what?" He would play along. He liked games. They

usually worked out in his favor.

"Are you going to stand there all night? Or make yourself useful?"

He stepped forward, oddly flat-footed. He usually had no trouble making himself useful to a woman—in a wide and imaginative variety of ways, if he said so himself—but with this woman he was flummoxed. "I'm not sure where to start." Sometimes the truth worked best.

She heaved a great sigh and tipped her head to the side. "You're not a stagehand, are you?"

"Erm, no."

Annoyance crossed her face. "No matter. You have hands, don't you?"

He held them up and rotated as if putting them on display for a prospective buyer.

"Surely you can use them to unknot this dreadful corset," she said, exasperated.

"I see nothing dreadful about your corset."

In fact, the corset did amazing things for what was a stunning figure. Emphasizing the curves of her waist. Rounding the generous mounds of her bosom.

She snorted. "You don't have to try breathing in it, do you?"

"*Touché.*"

She stood, back still to him, and placed her palms flat on the dressing table. He closed the distance separating them, thinking perhaps he shouldn't. This interaction wasn't proceeding at all how he would've liked.

He stopped three feet from her and contemplated the rather dauntingly complex system of laces and knots. This corset must date back to the 1750s, well before his time of unknotting ladies' corsets, which these days were simple stays.

"I'm afraid this may be well outside my level of expertise," he confessed, buying time, really. For here was the thing: if he began tugging one knot open, then another, and another, he wouldn't stop until he had the garment on the floor and convinced La

Contessa to join him in his bed—or against that wall over there.

"Then what use are you?" she huffed.

Oh, she really didn't want an answer to that question. He gave her the answer that fit within the bounds of propriety. "Not much, according to more than a few people."

Her head canted, and again her gaze met his in the mirror. "You're a proper nob, aren't you?"

"I don't know about the proper part."

Her gaze narrowed. Clearly, her mind was running a calculation, and one and one weren't making two. "What are you doing here?"

"Enjoying an evening's entertainment."

She shook her head. *"Here…*with *me."*

Now, they were getting somewhere.

"As it turns out, I'm here to ask a very similar question of you." He made her wait a few ticks of time. "What are *you* doing here? End of."

Chapter Two

VALENTINA PIVOTED AND faced the nob. With his blonde hair nearly the color of platinum and eyes that called to mind skies of vast clear blue, he looked like an angel. Even his evening coat was pure white.

Then one peered into those clear blue eyes.

And one realized if he was an angel, he was a fallen one.

Further, an unpredictable energy shimmered about this fallen angel.

He was going to foil the finely laid plans that had led her to the Five Graces.

She could sense it.

Though she didn't yet know his name, she already resented this lord. It was the way his mouth tipped into half a smile and the assurance that shone in his eyes. This lord was very accustomed to getting his way.

And it occurred to her: she didn't have to answer his question. The *why*'s of her life were none of his concern.

"I must change into my next costume, so if you will please..." She shooed him away as one would a pesky fly. She'd miss her mark if she didn't hurry, which would be the fifth time tonight. Which would get her a good yelling-at. *Again.*

The nob's feet remained planted, and his smile didn't slip a notch. "Why are you singing at the Five Graces?"

Truly, aristocrats could be incredibly stupid. "Why does anyone seek employment?" she asked, fumbling at her back for corset stays. He truly had no understanding of her world. *"Money."* She gave up on the corset and slipped a man's shirt over her head.

The nob continued staring at her, assessing. "But you're special."

She pulled up short, even as gratification snuck through her. Gratification she immediately suppressed. "I'm not special at all," she said, jerking a pair of trousers up her legs. She was to play a lad in the next comedy bit.

The nob opened his mouth, looking for all the world intent on contradicting her, when Mr. Degrass, the Five Graces' owner, shoved his massive girth behind the screen that Valentina had insisted upon for privacy. His gaze flicked toward the nob, and an obsequious smile spread across his face. "Why, Lord Archer, what a pleasant surprise to find you here. Are you enjoying the evening's entertainments?"

Lord Archer. She'd known it.

"I am, indeed," said Lord Archer.

Mr. Degrass's smile fell when it landed on Valentina. "Change of plan."

"Oh?" She was hastily tucking shirt into trousers.

"Put on this dress." He tossed her a garment.

Valentina held up the flimsy scrap of fabric. "But this isn't a dress," she said, slowly. "It's a chemise."

"Well, put it on, and be ready to go out again in five minutes."

"I'll need the dress," she said, a suspicion creeping in.

"That is the dress."

Just as she'd suspected. *"This* is an undergarment."

She glanced at Lord Archer, for some reason embarrassed that he was witnessing this exchange. His smile had disappeared, and in its place was a face like thunder.

"You can't have her go on the stage like that." His voice brooked no opposition.

Mr. Degrass gave Lord Archer his most patronizing smile. In the three days that Valentina had worked at the Five Graces, she'd come to know it well. "Lord Archer," he began, "now you go back to your seat with Lord Kilmuir and enjoy the rest of the show. Leave the talent to me. I know how to handle this chit."

Lord Archer's gaze swung toward Valentina. "You don't have to do what he says. You're worth more than that."

"What do you know of my worth?" she asked, exasperated.

"Only what I saw on stage. You were spectacular."

"And that's why we need to get her back on stage." Mr. Degrass pointed out. "Wearing *that*."

Lord Archer shook his head, implacable. "With her talent, that's hardly necessary."

"Who's talkin' *necessary*?" A laugh rumbled from the great depths of Mr. Degrass's belly. "I'm talkin' coin, milord. I mean, just look at her."

Lord Archer's gaze shifted toward Valentina and gave her a slow up-and-down that sent heat flushing through her. *Appreciation*, that was what she saw in his eyes. Since the age of sixteen, when her bosom had made its rather sudden and generous appearance, she'd been accustomed to such a look from the male gaze. She simply had that sort of figure and face. Mr. Degrass wasn't saying anything she hadn't half expected to hear.

But something more in Lord Archer's gaze had a feeling stealing through her. A new feeling. It sparked through her all warm and light and slightly tingly.

"She won't do it," said Lord Archer with firm finality.

"I won't?" snapped Valentina. She'd about had it with this nob sticking his nose into her affairs. "How dare you."

A single blonde eyebrow lifted with surprise. "So, you will do it?"

"I most definitely won't," she returned. "But that's for me and Mr. Degrass to sort out."

"Well, I say you will," blustered Mr. Degrass. "Or...or..."

Valentina's hands clenched at her sides, and she braced herself. Lord Archer had pushed the man into a corner, and there was but one way for him to save face.

"Or you can find yourself another theater," he finished.

No, no, no. Valentina spread her hands wide in supplication. "Surely, we can come to a mutual agreement."

"Then she shall leave," said Lord Archer.

"And good riddance," said Mr. Degrass. "The chit is more trouble than she's worth with her uppity airs. Demandin' a screen to change behind. Too good to show a bit of skin for a load of blunt."

"Hey!" protested Valentina.

But it was no use. Mr. Degrass continued, "Collect what you brought, and it's out through the stage door with you."

Seeing that her now-former employer was utterly serious, Valentina stuffed her dress and the few sundries she'd brought with her into a worn travel bag and found herself in a fetid alleyway, the door firmly closed behind her, in fewer than a handful of minutes. She exhaled a tiny roar of frustration.

Now what?

"What I don't understand," came an aristocratic voice behind her, "is why you're so upset."

Valentina swung around to find the source of her frustration—*Lord Archer*—propped against a wall, looking for all the world like he didn't have a care in the world.

Well, he didn't, did he?

Her mouth opened and closed, but words refused to emerge. What sheer, brazen, presumptuous gall!

He continued. "You can sing anywhere you want."

Her voice found itself. "How dare you."

"You're repeating yourself."

She could stamp her foot. That was how frustrating the man was. "You can't simply charge into someone's life and upend all their carefully laid plans."

For that was the thing—the Five Graces had figured prominently into her plans. Lords were known to frequent the place. Lords like the one before her.

Except not this lord at all.

A different lord.

Her job at the Five Graces had only been the beginning, and now this...this...*nob* had set her plans ablaze before they could gain a footing.

"As I see it," continued Lord Archer with breathtakingly supreme confidence, "I've done you a favor."

Valentina's mouth fell agape. The arrogance!

Lord Archer pushed off the wall. Valentina hoped it had left a smudge of dirt on his white superfine coat. Really, though, what sort of man wore white for a night in Southwark?

This sort, apparently.

Lord Archer.

"Now, you'll change out of those trousers, as fetching as they are on you," he said with a wink, "and put on that dress in your bag."

"Why would I do that?"

Oh, why had she asked? She was being drawn in, and she should resist with all her might. This entitled lord was entirely too accustomed to getting his way.

"Because you're coming with me."

A dry laugh escaped her. "I'm going nowhere with you."

His head cocked. "It's near midnight in Southwark, and you've lost your place of employment. Where else will you go?"

"Lord Archer—"

"Archie," he corrected. "Everyone who knows me calls me Archie."

"Well, see? That's the thing. I don't know you."

"You will after tonight, so we may as well skip the formalities."

She snorted. Could this man possibly be real? "Why are you taking an interest in me?"

"Because, Contessa—"

"Valentina," she said before immediately correcting herself. "Miss Hart."

"Miss Valentina Hart?" His ever-present smile widened. "Truly?"

"Truly," she said. "English father. Italian mother."

"Ah."

"You still haven't answered my question, Lord Archer."

"Because you have exceptional talent, Miss Hart. Your singing voice... How did you come by it?" For all his glib appearance, she detected true interest.

She shrugged. "I've always sung. My mother encouraged it." Why was she telling him all this? "Now, I shall be going."

"Where?"

"That's none of your concern."

"I'm afraid it is," he said, spreading his hands wide in apology—an apology that didn't reach his eyes.

"Why is that?" she asked, wary.

"Because I got you dismissed, and now you're my responsibility."

"The first part is true, but not the second."

Her words found no purchase with him. "Now you're going to put on the dress in your bag and come with me." When she didn't move, he continued, "Or we can stand in this alleyway all night. Though I'm certain the rats will have something to say about that eventually."

Rats. Ugh.

He turned his back to her and began whistling as he waited. She hesitated. If she put on that dress, then she would be as good as saying *yes* to whatever night he had planned. This Lord Archer, he possessed a wildness in his eyes that she didn't entirely trust. And yet, strangely, she didn't sense any real harm in him, either.

Really, all she had to do was see the night through until dawn, then she could begin reassessing her plans.

On a deep exhale, she exchanged one set of clothes for another and cleared her throat when she was presentable. He turned and gave her another up-and-down. "That'll do."

She laughed, utterly bemused. She'd never met anyone like this man.

"Now, I know just the place to lift your spirits."

Valentina wasn't sure she liked the sound of that, but she could see she hadn't much choice, either.

Through a maze of stinking, ill-lit alleyways and streets he led her, never once making a wrong turn. This lord who surely lived in Mayfair was too familiar with all the twists and turns of Southwark. More so than her, which wasn't saying much. She hailed miles from these parts, just outside London.

Soon, they'd stopped before a building that had all manner of people flurrying in and out of its front door. "Here we are," he said with a flourish.

"This isn't a brothel, is it?" She'd assured Mama no brothels.

He laughed and shook his head. "Chaz's is only a hell."

"A *hell?*" That didn't sound any better.

"A gaming hell," he said, digging into the interior pocket of his coat. "You see, Miss Hart, what you need is a few tosses of the dice."

"I'm not sure that's true." In fact, she was certain it wasn't.

"And you'll do it with this."

He extended a small pouch and pressed it into her palm. The pouch jingled. "Is this coin?"

"As good as," he said.

"Pardon?" In her world, nothing was *as good as* blunt. Only blunt was blunt.

"They're markers, which you'll use in place of actual money."

"I cannot possibly accept this." She tried to return the pouch.

He stepped back, hands up as if warding off plague. "You can, and you shall. Think of it as seed money."

"Seed money?" It felt like real money to her.

"Whatever you win in Chaz's, you can keep."

That drew Valentina up short. "I can *keep?*"

He nodded.

"My winnings?"

He smiled.

"All of them?"

"You have my word."

And therein lay the problem. "I haven't the faintest idea what your word is worth."

"As a gentleman."

She almost snorted. "In my experience, it's the gentlemen you need to keep the closest eye on."

Recent, painful experience. Experience that had led her to the Five Graces, in fact.

"Not this gentleman."

Irritatingly, inconceivably, she believed him. Likely because of those clear blue eyes that appeared as if they'd never told a lie.

Now the look in those eyes…

That was a different story.

That look was decidedly devilish.

A man of contradictions, this Lord Archer.

"Now, shall we?" He held out his arm for her.

She hesitated. If she took his arm, she was committing to this folly. Then she tested the weight of the pouch. What harm could there be in it? With these markers, she might be able to repair the damage that had been done tonight and recover her family's savings altogether. Then there would be no need for the other plan that had involved the Five Graces.

She took Lord Archer's arm. She couldn't help but test the solidity beneath her palm. Quite a few muscles lay beneath white superfine. Surprising, that. And he smelled… *Delicious.* Like spice cake. How could a man possibly smell so good?

They stepped inside Chaz's gaming hell, and just before the raucous atmosphere swallowed them whole, Valentina's gaze swept the room littered with all manner of tables, lively patrons trying their luck. "Which games require no skill?" she asked.

"Hazard." Lord Archer indicated a table in a far corner. "And roulette." He gestured toward a closer table.

Valentina liked the look of the spinning wheel. "Roulette," she decided.

She approached the table and dug into the pouch, finding a marker. She plunked it onto crimson felt, even as she felt Lord Archer's presence at her back. The croupier simply stared at her.

"Assign it a value," Lord Archer said into her ear.

"Like?"

"Five guineas," he said around her. "Now," he continued, "you can place the markers anywhere you like. On numbers. On the corners of numbers. On red or black. On red *and* black, if you like even odds. I suggest sitting this one out and watching the other players. You'll catch the gist of it."

As these seemed like the first reasonable words to emerge from Lord Archer's mouth all night, Valentina listened and watched and, indeed, caught on.

"Lucky number seven," called out the croupier after the white marble had hopped wildly around the wheel, eventually nesting into the 7 slot. Groans sounded all around the table, save from the one person who had played red. No one had played 7.

Valentina slid a few markers toward 7.

"Are you certain?" asked Lord Archer. "That number just came up."

"I don't see any reason why it shouldn't come up again," she said. "Every spin is a new beginning."

"I like your way of thinking, Miss Hart," said Lord Archer.

Truly, he was unlike any man Valentina had met in all her twenty years. Of course, she wasn't acquainted with many—or any—aristocrats. Perhaps they were all like him—just a little mad.

Bets were placed, and the croupier again spun the wheel and set the small white marble into motion, which whirred in the opposite direction of the wheel, eventually slowing as it bounced from one number to the next. As patrons shouted for their numbers or colors to come up, Valentina stood, mouth pressed into a firm line, hands clutching the edge of the table. While this was fun for everyone else in the room, it was serious business for her.

If she won, she would be that much closer to recovering Papa's savings and clearing his mounting debts.

Her gaze fixed, the white marble skipped once...twice...then plopped into a slot. A roar rattled the rafters, and Valentina blinked, unable to believe her eyes.

7.

Impossibly, the marble had landed on 7. The croupier cleared the table of all but her markers, then slid a rather sizable pile her way.

"Well played," came Lord Archer's voice.

A shiver slipped through Valentina. She wasn't sure if it was the thrill of victory.

Or his praise, spoken low and velvet in her ear.

Or something else... Something she couldn't rightly identify.

She shook the thought away and accepted her winnings, her blood soaring with triumph and possibility. If she could do that— her mind did a quick calculation—ten more times, she would have Papa's finances settled and forget the other scheme she'd had planned.

"Want to try your luck at hazard?" asked Lord Archer.

"Not a chance," she said, determined.

She experienced a feeling she hadn't felt in months. *Hope.*

Here at Chaz's gaming hell, tonight, at this roulette table, she was going to fix what had gone so desperately wrong for her family.

She might have to allow that it would be thanks to Lord Archer.

She'd keep that last bit to herself.

Chapter Three

ARCHIE STEPPED BACK and observed Miss Valentina Hart as she gambled on roulette like she really meant it.

He'd only brought her here as a lark, to get her mind off having just lost her employment. Of course, her place at the Five Graces was no great loss. She could do better, though, curiously, she didn't seem to understand that.

On the next spin of the wheel, she lost the number—*44*—but won the color—*black*—the one gain more than offsetting the other loss. Then another spin, and another win—the corner of 18. Did the woman possess a prescience that made her particularly skilled at this game of whirling luck?

After her fifth win in a row, she tossed him a smile. Eyes bright, a dimple in her left cheek, he sensed daring in that smile. A daring that pushed through her natural reserve.

A daring that called to a place in him that had no choice but to respond. "You're wilder than you think, you know," he couldn't help saying.

She tossed a laugh his way and played on, wild and daring, for a length of time that was impossible to track within the timeless confines of a gaming hell. Certainly, she lost here and there, but mostly she won and won and won.

Then it started.

She began losing.

Once was a fluke.

Twice was a bit of bad luck.

Thrice was a pattern.

Dame Fortune had, at last, deserted her. It had been bound to happen, as it did to every gambler. Miss Hart, however, hadn't yet learned that hard fact and kept throwing money at the problem. Archie sensed in his gut it would only get worse from here.

Her smile fell with each spin of the wheel, the crease between her eyebrows deepening. When she was down to two markers, her gaze flicked toward him, then skittered away. But the contact lasted long enough for him to catch an emotion in there.

Panic.

Odd, that. What did Miss Hart have to be panicked about? She wasn't gambling with her own money. But the way she was behaving... It was as if she were.

She placed her markers on red, her shoulders set in the posture of someone holding her breath while the wheel spun. The marble skittered and hopped until, at last, finding a home—*8*.

Black.

She gasped and went stone still.

"Shall we try our luck at the hazard table?" he asked. He needed to pry her away from roulette.

She shook her head, silent, body tensed with held breath.

Something was wrong. *Very* wrong. More wrong than simply losing a few guineas at roulette. "Miss Hart, perhaps it would be best if we—"

Then she exhaled a great heave of breath and along with it a great, wet sob. Here, at Chaz's roulette table, the woman began weeping. "Oh, why can nothing go right?" she blubbered.

Archie took Miss Hart by the shoulders and met her square in the eyes. What he saw there weren't tears of sadness or loss, but rather tears of anger and frustration.

Right.

He wrapped his hand around her upper arm and set a brisk pace as he marched her outside and down the street, the first golden rays of dawn streaking across the morning sky. He pulled her into the first deserted alcove they came to and made her face him.

"Now," he said, stern, "what the devil is going on? Tell me." He could deliver a lordly command when circumstances called for it. Like now.

She swiped tears away with the back of her hand and sniffled. "I don't have to tell you anything."

Archie wasn't particularly bothered. He had experience in dealing with stubborn females—namely two stubborn sisters and a stubborn cousin, to boot. "You see, I have a basic inability to stay out of other people's business. Let's start with the simplest question first. Why were you on the Five Graces stage pretending to be an Italian contessa?"

The woman before him suddenly looked tired and vulnerable, wearied not simply by a long night and a great explosion of emotion, but by life itself. He sensed a relenting in her.

"So the *haute ton* will let me sing for it."

His brow lifted in surprise. "Why? For money? Is that why you were playing roulette as if your life depended on it? If that's all you need, then go to Paris or Italy and open your mouth. You'll be a sensation overnight."

She shook her head. She looked...*defeated*. Archie didn't like that one single bit.

"I need to gain entry into a room with someone in London," she said.

"Someone?"

"A man."

"A man?" He would stand here all day and pry the entire story from her word by word, if that was what it took. "Forgive my forwardness, but with your looks, you could find yourself in a room with any man you like with a crook of your little finger."

She exhaled a wearied sigh. "A lord."

"My statement stands."

Miss Hart rolled her eyes toward the brightening sky. *Good.* It felt right that her spunk was returning.

"At the risk of sounding repetitive," he said, "I'll ask again. *Why?*"

Her gaze followed the slow, lumbering progress of a donkey cart. Archie didn't think she would answer. Then she said, "My father is an apothecary, from a long line of apothecaries. With each generation, the business has become more successful. Papa was approached by a lord with an opportunity."

She appeared to be bracing herself for what came next. Archie felt himself doing the same.

"This lord knew for a fact that the royal apothecary would be going into retirement soon. If Papa wanted his name considered for the position, this lord would mention him." Her jaw clenched and released. "For a small fee."

Archie saw how this would go. "Which wasn't small for anyone not an aristocrat."

She nodded. "Large enough to put a business in danger of bankruptcy."

"But it would be worth it to secure royal patronage."

"Which the lord guaranteed."

"He took your father's money."

"And Papa never heard from him again. Then…"

"Then?"

"Papa was at the pub one night and overheard a stonemason telling the same story. They soon learned this lord had been playing this same swindle on men from various professions throughout the countryside. But they also knew there was nothing they could do about it."

"Why is that?"

She tossed him a bitter smile. "Because lords are untouchable, *my lord.*"

Archie felt the sting of her barb. But what stung most was that she wasn't wrong. Still, he had a question. "How does that add up to you singing at the Five Graces?"

"I had to do something."

"I can't imagine that would afford you enough money to save your father from debtor's prison."

"The Five Graces was only the first part of my plan."

Her mouth clamped shut. It was clear she wasn't going to tell him the rest right now. No matter. They could get to that later.

For now, he had another question. "What is this lord's name?"

"Lord Nestor."

Reflexively, Archie's jaw tensed.

Miss Hart's gaze narrowed on him. "You know this lord?"

"I have that particular misfortune."

"Let me guess. You've been friends since childhood."

"*Friends* would be overstating the relationship."

"You don't like him."

"I don't." That was putting it mildly. It was almost too much information at once, and he realized they both needed a rest. "Can I drop you home?"

"Home is several miles north, Hampstead village." She shifted on her feet. "Mr. Degrass allowed me a cot backstage at the Five Graces."

That made up Archie's mind. "You're coming with me."

She canted her head. "Is life always like this with you?"

"Like what?"

"A complete whirlwind."

Archie didn't even have to think. "Yes."

He left her standing on the cobblestone sidewalk, mouth slightly agape, as he stepped to the street and flagged down a hackney with a short, sharp whistle. Soon after, they'd settled onto opposite benches in the conveyance, her eyes fluttered shut and she drifted off to sleep, giving him room for thought.

Was he taking this matter too far?

Possibly.

But didn't he take everything too far? Wasn't he known for it?

This woman—*Miss Valentina Hart*—she was the first breath of inspiration he'd experienced in months. He mustn't let his muse slip away. But...

How far would he go for inspiration?

That wasn't the correct question.

How far *wouldn't* he go?

Half an hour later, they arrived at Casa Windermere, the family's mansion in Mayfair. He tapped Miss Hart's knee as they approached. She startled awake, her eyes wide as she attempted to orient herself.

"We've arrived," he said. "You shall stay here until we get you all sorted."

She blinked and gathered her wits. "I'm not yours to sort."

He shrugged, uninterested in arguing the point.

He stepped down from the carriage and held out his hand to help her alight. She hesitated a moment before placing her hand in his.

He understood why the instant she did—as a responding spark blazed through him.

This taking of her hand felt suspiciously—remarkably—like an intimacy.

Then her feet were on the ground, and he was holding her hand two heartbeats too long, and his gaze had settled on that ruby-red, made-for-sin mouth of hers.

His grip relented, and she snatched her hand back as if singed. Her eyes wanted to know what had just happened, and his body wanted to show her.

Right.

He was halfway to a cockstand.

Right.

He cleared his throat. "My sister's lady's maid Tucker will assist you with all your needs."

He bowed and pivoted on his heel, leaving Miss Hart to the care of servants as he made his way to his study.

All of her needs?

He could think of a few he could help with, for she radiated a luscious sensuality that looked primed to be awakened.

No.

He must cease these thoughts. The woman needed his help, and that was all. He wasn't a heartless rake, but a Windermere, a little wild, yes, but noble.

It was time he started thinking like it.

Chapter Four

Later

VALENTINA EXTENDED HER arms overhead and felt a smile widen across her face as every muscle in her body lengthened in the most luxurious stretch of her life.

She froze, and her eyes flew open.

This wasn't a dream.

She was really, truly luxuriating in the most comfortable bed she'd ever laid bottom upon, soft down feathers and crisp cotton sheets below her, a diaphanous coral canopy above. With bright sun filtering through ivory curtains, the room was soothing and lovely and not at all where she should be.

Judging by the light filtering through the sheer curtains, it was well past midday. Which meant she'd been sleeping here for hours.

And the man who had brought her here… Where was he?

A sound drifted through the air. *Music.* Piano music, to be precise. It was lovely, simple on the surface, but possessed of a depth that had her humming a melody on top of it. As if this bed and this room needed to be made more heavenly.

The music suddenly stopped, and Valentina snapped to, sweeping the bedcovers aside and hopping from the bed. She caught her reflection in the dressing table mirror. Remarkably, she didn't look a fright. In fact, she might look well-rested. She grabbed her gray cotton dress draped across the bench. It had been pressed and—she lifted it to her nose—scented faintly with rosewater.

Last night returned to her in a blur. She'd lost her place at the Five Graces, leaving her plan in shambles. Then she'd gambled away her one chance to salvage the loss. All because of one man.

Lord Archer.

The man in whose bed she'd slept.

Well, not *his* bed, but close enough.

All the light, frothy elegance surrounding her was *his*.

She needed to leg it out of here.

She dressed quickly, ran an ivory comb through her hair, and snatched up her travel bag. The door opened on silent hinges, and she poked her head out, checking that no one was about. Corridor empty, she slipped across black-and-white checkered marble. When she reached the head of the staircase, again she glanced about to make sure she was alone, then she rapidly descended the stairs, the wide double front door now in her sights. All she had to do was cross the twenty-foot width of the receiving hall, and she would be through the door with nary a look back.

Perhaps it was rude to leave without thanking Lord Archer for his hospitality, but she couldn't see any other way. She couldn't afford to be involved with someone like him—someone who would only complicate her life further.

She had enough complications—like figuring out another way to secure her family's lost savings.

Of a sudden, the front door swung open and in strode a large and quite handsome man with a head of reddish gold hair and bright blue eyes. The half-smile that was already on his face widened. "You are Miss Hart," he said with a small bow.

That bow said all she needed to know about him. *Another lord.* Heaven help her. These lords kept blocking her way at every turn.

"I am," she said, irritated and pettish. "Are we acquainted?"

"I watched you sing last night at the Five Graces. So, I reckon we could say 'tis I who is acquainted with you, but you don't know me from Adam. Lord Kilmuir," he finished with another bow.

Valentina nodded and said, "Nice to make your acquaintance, milord."

It wasn't, but her manners hadn't entirely abandoned her.

"Are you looking for the morning room?"

"Actually, I'm looking for the front door."

He blinked, then laughed. He thought she was being funny. He held out his arm and said, "Come with me."

Valentina saw she had no choice. As he guided her through the house, she noticed that every room in this mansion contained large windows that allowed light to pour in, creating a bright, airy house—an inviting house. Just the sort of house that seemed perfect for a man like Lord Archer.

Annoying thought, that one.

Lord Kilmuir led her into a room that overlooked a garden in full June blossom. In front of the bow window sat Lord Archer at a round table with two other ladies, all bathed in golden light. One of the women looked very similar to Lord Archer with her platinum curls that just brushed her shoulders and blue eyes that held no small amount of mischief. She must be a sister. The other woman looked very similar to the others, but her hair was raven black and her eyes green and quietly observant. A more gorgeous trio of people Valentina had never beheld—almost too gorgeous to behold directly.

Upon Valentina and Lord Kilmuir's entrance, Lord Archer shot to his feet and began making introductions. "Miss Hart, may I introduce you to my sister Lady Delilah and our cousin Miss Windermere?"

A tight smile formed about Valentina's mouth. "Delighted to make your acquaintance."

The ladies' heads tipped subtly to the side as they took her in. Valentina shifted on her feet, suddenly too aware of how she and her presence here must appear. A right hoyden, sleeping in strange men's houses. That was what they were surely thinking of her. Oh, she needed to vacate this house.

"You won't meet our other sister, Lady Amelia, today," said Lord Archer, resuming his seat.

"I believe it's more correct to call her the Duchess of Ripon," said Miss Windermere.

"She ran off with a duke last year," explained Lord Archer.

"Then insisted on marrying him," said Lady Delilah.

"And living with him," added Miss Windermere.

Lord Archer spread his hands wide in apology. "Hence her absence from midday tea."

Lady Delilah stood—oh, but she was tall and willowy—and indicated the chair to her left. "Miss Hart, perhaps you can talk some sense into my brother."

"I sincerely doubt that," said Valentina without thinking.

Lady Delilah laughed. "I already like her, Archie," she said to her brother before returning the full intensity of her gaze to Valentina. "It's simply that I've been presented with the opportunity to acquire a pet."

"A pet?"

She nodded, her curls bouncing. "A pet baby goat, to be precise."

"Delilah, not this again," said Lord Archer with a roll of his eyes.

"Perhaps our guest can offer a new perspective." Lady Delilah's gaze settled on Valentina. "What do you think of a goat as a pet?"

"I think it's a terrible idea," said Valentina. She had nothing to lose by being honest.

Lord Kilmuir began coughing up the swallow of tea he'd just taken, and Miss Windermere smiled as if holding back a giggle.

Lady Delilah looked no small bit exasperated. "And why is that?"

Valentina pointed toward the garden outside the window. "Do you like that garden?" All manner of roses, peonies, hollyhocks, and daisies blossomed in the garden, colors bursting in brilliant white, red, pink, yellow, purple, and blue.

"I do," said Lady Delilah.

"Baby goats grow into adult goats, and an adult goat will eat it clean in a week."

A Windermere family quality was becoming clear to Valentina. They were big on ideas, but not so much when it came to pragmatics.

Lady Delilah's eyebrows creased and released. "Ah." She glanced at her brother. "No need to gloat, Archie."

He spread his hands wide. "I didn't say a word."

"You didn't need to."

"Well, I must say," said Miss Windermere, "those are quite the most sensible words spoken in this house since Aunt and Uncle left for Denmark."

"Denmark?" asked Valentina, unable to help herself.

Lady Delilah gave a little shrug. "Oh, our parents are absolutely mad about digging up old bones and ruins in foreign lands. Vikings are the latest obsession."

Somehow, Valentina felt herself becoming drawn into the Windermere world. They possessed an irresistibility.

Yet she must resist.

She must speak her thank-yous and farewells and consign this strange interlude to a passing folly.

Then food and drink were served, and she found herself eating and drinking, and not leaving.

Lord Archer caught her eye. "I have a plan."

She froze mid-chew. "What plan?" she asked around the scone in her mouth.

No one seemed at all surprised by this non sequitur. Which could only mean one thing: everyone had been apprised of her and her family's plight.

Oh, bother.

The bite of scone turned to sawdust in her mouth, and she swallowed with some difficulty. "That is completely unnecessary,

Lord Archer. I have a plan, and it was going very well until—"

"Until?"

"Until I met you."

A few ticks of time beat by before Lord Archer sat back in his chair and laughed. "That's very funny, Miss Hart. Now, tell us your plan."

Valentina felt as if she'd been backed into a tight corner, her only option to fight her way out. She held Lord Archer's gaze and said, "I don't have to."

"She has you there, Arch," said Lady Delilah.

Valentina sensed a possible ally.

"Oh, come now," said Lord Archer.

For reasons entirely unknown to her, Valentina relented. "My plan is—*was*—to work my way up to singing for the *ton*."

The frustrating man nodded, as if considering her plan. "You do have the talent," he said slowly. "So, to be clear, your plan is to get into a room with Lord Nestor."

"A public one." A vital piece of the plan.

"Then what?" asked Lord Archer, serious. More serious than she'd thought him capable. "Ask him very nicely to return your father's money?"

Discomfort stole through Valentina, her footing slightly less firm than it had been a moment ago. It felt as if Lord Archer were setting her up. "I won't be nice about it," she said, defensive, which she didn't like.

"Again, to be clear," began Lord Archer, somehow intruding into her space from all the way across the table. Such was the intensity of his gaze. "Your plan is to publicly shame and humiliate a lord in front of his peers?"

Valentina nodded. "He will have to return our money."

She'd thought this plan through and knew it to be perfect, but the four pairs of eyes staring at her seemed to have reached a very different conclusion. She thought she might even see pity.

Of course, it was Lord Archer who would open his mouth to point out whatever fatal flaw she'd missed.

Valentina braced herself.

⚔️

ARCHIE GLANCED AROUND the room. "Everyone leave." When Miss Hart made to stand, he said, "Not you."

What he needed to say was for her ears only. He had no desire to cause her embarrassment.

As Delilah exited the room, she said over her shoulder, "Whatever plan you're hatching, Archie, make sure I'm part of it. Nestor is a nasty piece of work."

Now that he and Miss Hart were alone, he could observe her in the daylight. As beautiful as she'd been in the shadow of night, it was nothing to her beauty in the full light of day.

But he hadn't cleared the room to do what he usually did when he found himself alone with a beautiful woman—namely to set about seducing her.

He was here to help her.

Not help himself *to* her.

"Here's what will happen," he began, his voice steady and utterly serious. "After you throw your accusations around in front of all the *ton*, the room will go dead silent. You will never have heard a silence like it. Then Lord Nestor will rise to his feet in the stately manner he perfected while still in leading strings, and with a confused smile on his face, he will say he's never had dealings with this woman—*you*—in his life. Which you will have to admit is true, because you, dearest Contessa, are a terrible liar."

"Now wait a minute," she protested.

He held up a staying hand. "We both know it." He continued. "Lord Nestor will ask the room to listen to the 'contessa' speak. *She's no contessa*, he will say. *Her accent is pure English countryside.* Then he will deliver the death blow to your plan. He will accuse you of being the fraud in the room and of trying to extort money from a peer of the realm."

A dusky pink blush stained Miss Hart's high cheekbones as

her face transformed with pure outrage.

Before she could open her mouth to give it voice, Archie continued. "The room full of peers of the realm won't take kindly to the accusation, and it'll be off to the Old Bailey with you. And you're too lovely for a place like that."

Miss Hart's shoulders sagged ever so slightly. She truly hadn't thought her plan through. Archie admired her fire and passion and didn't like that he'd been the one to dampen them.

Why had he added the last bit, though?

Because it was the truth. She *was* lovely.

Now that he'd told her the disheartening bit, it was time for the fun bit. "There is only one way to squeeze blunt from a swindler."

She didn't want to ask what. That was what her eyes were telling him, but how could she not? At last, she exhaled a long-suffering sigh. "I'm waiting."

Archie smiled. "It's simple. You outswindle him."

"I wouldn't know the first thing about orchestrating a swindle."

"It's a good thing you have me."

"I...*have*...you?"

"There are worse things."

"Such as?"

He wouldn't dignify the question with an answer. "Listen, I don't have anything on the calendar for the next fortnight or so." Or for the next year or so. "It'll be a lark."

Her eyes narrowed. He'd pushed it too far. "A lark?" she asked, incredulous. "You expect me to place my family's future in the hands of a man who considers it to be nothing more than a lark?"

He spread his hands wide. "I'm afraid you haven't much of a choice."

He had her. But he wouldn't gloat. In fact, he felt quite serious about the whole thing.

And it was serious words that next flowed from his mouth. "I won't let you down."

The words did nothing to displace the skepticism in her eyes. He didn't like that. For some reason, he wanted this woman to believe in him—to trust in him.

"If I fail you—" He thought fast. *What to say... What to say...* The magic words came to him. "I shall repay what your father and the others lost."

A frown pulled at the corners of her mouth. "*You?* Why would you do that?"

Archie made himself shrug, striving for his usual glib indifference. "I've lost more in a single night in the hells of the rookeries, I can assure you."

It wasn't true, but it was what this woman would think of an aristocrat.

She didn't relent. "I find that mildly insulting." Her head canted. "What sort of a lord are you, anyway?"

"Not much of one. Just ask around."

This pulled a dry laugh from her. He liked making her laugh.

"Truly, I'm your best hope for revenge," he said, hoping that laugh had cracked open a door he could slip inside.

"I'm not out for revenge, Lord Archer. Only what's owed my family."

"But don't you want revenge, too? Just a little?"

She was tempted to say *yes*. He could see it in her expressive eyes. He liked tempting her.

"We can get your money *and* revenge in one fell swoop."

"And what do you get out of it, Lord Archer?"

Archie's shoulder lifted in the unbothered shrug he'd mastered by age five. The one that led people away from truths he didn't want to reveal. "A lark," he said. "Besting Nestor."

It wasn't that these weren't truths. It was just that they were small truths.

Spending more time with you, my muse.

That would've been the large truth.

"I really must insist that you let me help." He supposed he

couldn't force her to stay, but he was directing the full force of his renowned charm and persuasion her way.

A few seconds stretched slowly past before curiosity won out and she asked, "What's your plan?"

Archie could have jumped for joy. But he didn't. He remained firmly planted in his chair so as not to frighten Miss Hart away. As for the plan... "That's an interesting question," he said, buying himself a little time to think.

"You don't have one, do you?"

"Not as such, no." Sometimes the truth was the best path.

A laugh chirruped out of her, then another, and another. Then she was laughing and couldn't seem to help herself. Unable to let anyone laugh alone, Archie began laughing, too. "What is it that we're laughing about?" he finally asked.

"You..." she finally got out.

"Me?" He wasn't sure he liked the sound of that.

"You finally got me to agree to your plan, and you don't even have one."

Archie stopped laughing. "All we have to do is figure out how to extract five thousand pounds from Nestor."

He'd set the stage for a plan, at least. Surely she could appreciate that.

Finally, she stopped laughing. "Seems to me all you lords think about are your pleasures. So, what does he like?"

She rather had a point, even if it made him appear deep as a puddle of mud. "He likes gambling." *Too much.* That was known. "And women." Well, who didn't? "And—" *Ah.* Here it was. A smile creased his face. "You're a genius, Miss Hart." From a slight idea a plan began to form, but he needed to know something first. "Have you ever laid eyes on Nestor?"

"Once. From a distance."

"Describe him."

"Middling height."

Archie nodded.

"Dark hair."

Archie kept nodding. "From all the grease."

"Very light skin."

"Pasty is the word you're searching for, I believe."

"Perhaps on the heavy side."

"Protuberant backside?"

She nodded.

"Sounds like Nestor, but we must know for certain. Could be a swindler impersonating a lord." He doubted it, knowing what he did of Nestor's character, but it must be confirmed before they acted on any plan.

"And how do we make sure?"

Archie's gaze narrowed on Miss Hart. "You're quite a small woman, aren't you?"

"I'm large enough," she said defensively.

"But not too large, and that is rather the point."

"The point?"

He nodded. This could work. "We're off to Tattersall's."

"Tattersall's?" she asked. It was clear she'd never heard of the place.

"It's a horse market. There's only one thing Nestor likes more than fast women, and that's fast horses."

Miss Hart looked unconvinced.

"Unless you'd like to try the fast woman approach?"

"I think not."

"Fast horses, it is."

"Horses?"

"We are going to sell Nestor a racehorse."

"A racehorse?"

"A fictional one."

"Why?"

"Because an Arabian stallion can easily go for five thousand pounds, and we just so happen to know a lord who has that amount of blunt."

"And how do I and my...*small-ness*...fit into this scheme?" She looked as if she hadn't wanted to ask.

"Well, you don't. Not as you are anyway."

"Explain."

"Do you still have the trousers from last night in your possession?"

"Pardon?"

From the expression on her face, it looked as if it was occurring to Miss Hart that he might not simply be an eccentric lord, but one who was madder than a March hare.

His next words certainly wouldn't disabuse her of that impression.

"As my stable lad, you'll do quite nicely."

And with that, he stood. He'd always known when to make an exit. Miss Hart's flummoxed gaze fast upon him, he crossed the room and stopped at the open doorway. "Meet me at the foot of the stairs within the half hour. In your trousers," he added, as if that weren't already clear.

With that, he exited the room, leaving Miss Hart and her dumbfounded expression behind. A spring in his step, Archie felt utterly inspired and utterly alive for the first time in months.

Somehow, he'd convinced his muse to spend more time with him.

How could this afternoon be anything other than a lark?

Chapter Five

THE AFTERNOON WASN'T a lark.

It was a mistake.

Putting Miss Hart in trousers, that was.

Quite simply, Archie hadn't anticipated how fetching his muse would be in the attire of a stable lad.

How could he have?

Though she'd worn trousers last night, he hadn't gotten a proper view of her in them—or more precisely, a specific view of her in them.

From behind.

How could he have predicted how fetching a female bottom would be in a pair of trousers?

Miss Hart's female bottom.

He was giving himself a cockstand just thinking about it.

Which was why he had her trailing him like a good servant as they strolled Tattersall's subscription rooms and courtyard to see if Nestor was there. Every twenty or so steps, he stopped and greeted a friend or acquaintance, and Miss Hart stood discreetly away, hands clasped before her, eyes turned to the ground, as they'd agreed. She wasn't to make eye contact with anyone. She was entirely too pretty, and their ruse would be immediately discovered.

Not that Archie would suffer many consequences. In fact, the *ton* would expect such a jape from Lord Archer.

So, they'd agreed that when she spotted Nestor, she would give two quick tugs on his overcoat.

As they left the last subscription room, Archie knew he'd been wasting their time. There was but one place Nestor would be—the stables.

Miss Hart drew abreast with him. "I have a question for you," she said, low, for his ears only.

"Ask away," he said, nodding at a family acquaintance. Of course, ninety percent of the occupants of Tattersall's were acquaintances of the family or friend variety.

"Does someone in your household play the piano?"

If a question could command his full attention, that was the one. "All of us Windermeres took lessons as children," he said neutrally.

She shook her head. "Someone who could play in any music hall in England."

Though he walked, he felt a still concentration take hold of him. "Why do you ask?"

"I heard music before I came down to the morning room. Beautiful music," she added.

It was all he could do to maintain an air of indifference. "Perhaps a neighbor across the back garden was playing and the music drifted in with the breeze."

"Perhaps." That *perhaps* entirely lacked the ring of belief.

Though he tried to tamp it down, gratification soared through Archie. Miss Hart thought the music beautiful... She thought *his* music beautiful.

He was just about to press for her thoughts on the music—it was a fact that artists were a needy bunch—when her gaze shifted and widened. Then he felt it. Two sharp tugs on his overcoat. He knew before he followed the direction of her eyes.

Nestor.

There he stood, at the end of the row of horse stalls.

Further, the fact that Miss Hart had tugged on his coat at the sight of the man meant something. Lord Nestor was, indeed, the very lord who had swindled her father and countless others out of their savings.

The game was on.

"Follow my lead," said Archie.

Blithe smile on his face, he slowed his step to a leisurely amble down the row, giving each stallion, thoroughbred, and pony careful consideration, keeping Nestor in the periphery of his vision. He stopped a good ten feet from the man, close enough for Nestor to hear him, but far enough to acknowledge they weren't exactly on greeting terms.

There wasn't precisely a history between him and Nestor beyond the fact that Archie had simply never liked him, not at Eton or later at Cambridge or as adults in London. It was simply that Nestor had the presence of an oily shadow and navigated the world as such.

Archie cleared his throat. "What poor quality the horseflesh is today," he said loudly. "Nothing like what's arrived from Italy."

Nestor turned an assessing eye onto him. "What's this, Archer?" The man tried to sound disinterested—and failed.

Archie shifted on his feet. Who said Delilah was the only actor in the family? "I shouldn't be talking about it."

Nestor sidled closer. "What's a small confidence between old school chums?"

That was a stretch, and they both knew it, but civility demanded that Archie leave it be. That, and the fact that Archie was trying to outswindle the man.

He allowed a few beats of time to tick past, then he gave Nestor a conspiratorial half smile. "You know my sister, Lady Delilah, correct?"

"I believe she continues to labor under the impression that my name is Lord Fester."

Good old Delilah. Archie only just didn't snort. Miss Hart, however, wasn't as successful as she launched into a coughing fit, which had Nestor lifting an unimpressed eyebrow, implying Archie needed a firmer hand with his servant.

"Well, she made a friend in Italy," continued Archie, wishing Miss Hart would get a hold of herself. "A *contessa*, as it happens. You know the story—young beauty married to a titled, aging *roué*."

"A version of it, as it happens." Nestor didn't speak the words lightly, as a joke, but bitterly and with a sour twist to his mouth.

All the *ton* knew the story of how the elder Lord Nestor had gambled away the family's fortune before running off to the Continent with his mistress, where he'd perished within three years of the pox.

Archie gave a commiserative smile. "Well, the old count won an Arabian off a sultan in a card game. Then several months—and several hundred card games later—he lost a whole stable of horses, save one. Then he died, leaving behind a young, impoverished widow. Well, *la contessa* is in London." He waggled an eyebrow. "With the Arabian."

Nestor snorted. "Man or horse?" he asked drily.

"Horse."

"To breed or race?" asked Nestor. Archie sensed he was losing the man's interest.

"To *sell*," said Archie.

If Nestor had been a dog, his ears would have perked up. Archie could practically see the wheels turning inside the man's head. He glanced down at Miss Hart. Eyes fast on her feet, a subtle cant to her head, she was following every nuance of the conversation.

"Are you going to buy the horse?" asked Nestor.

Archie shrugged. "Considering it."

"Why wouldn't you? Everyone knows the Windermeres have the blunt." There it was again—the bitterness Nestor had carried with him all his life.

"In truth, I'm seeking a partner," said Archie, offhand. "I've recently come into monetary fluidity, erm, *issues*, and the contessa wants payment in solid guineas. And who has that sort of money readily available?"

"It so happens—" began Nestor.

Archie cut him off with a tip of his hat. "Nestor, I won't take up any more of your afternoon. Good day."

He pivoted on his heel and started walking. A flurry of rapid footsteps had Miss Hart beside him, shooting daggers at the side of his face. He met her panicked eyes with calm and began counting down. If he wasn't too far off the mark, Lord Nestor would be calling out in *five...four...three...*

"Archer!"

Archie pivoted and waited while the man caught up. Miss Hart looked mildly winded, unaccustomed to bluffing an opponent. "Yes?" he asked, the question dripping with utter indifference.

Nestor cleared his throat in the manner of one who wanted something very much, but didn't wish to appear so.

And that was when Archie knew he had him.

"It so happens I have a cache of blunt set aside," said Nestor, casual. Archie wondered if his palms were sweaty. Miss Hart's surely were. "Have you seen the horse?"

"In Italy."

"How old is it?"

"Two years."

"It can run?"

"Next year at Ascot, it will leave the field in its dust."

Nestor glanced about and lowered his voice. "Have you discussed the Arabian with anyone else?" he asked in a near whisper.

"Actually, I was just on my way to see Rakesley." The Duke of Rakesley was a known breeder of thoroughbreds. Four years running, a horse from his stable placed at Ascot, Doncaster, and Epsom. One would only approach Rakesley about serious horseflesh that could contend.

Nestor paled, looking utterly stricken. Then his fists clenched at his sides, and determination hardened about his mouth.

"You've found your man."

"Pardon?"

"Fifty-fifty."

"Let's not be hasty. I feel quite confident that Rakesley would appreciate the opportunity to invest. He does have one of the finest stables in the land."

Nestor shook his head, adamant. Archie understood this was serious business, that the future of several families hung in the balance, but, oh, this was fun.

"*We* could have one of the best stables in the land, Archer." If a whisper could be a shout, Nestor's was. "No other investors. I quite insist upon it."

Archie shrugged. "If you insist."

This was going easier than he'd dreamed possible.

Too easy.

He didn't trust anything that was too easy.

Anything worth having offered up a bit of resistance. It must be striven for.

"Of course," he found himself saying, "you'll have to meet the contessa."

Just behind him came a muffled feminine squeak.

This was, indeed, fun.

VALENTINA COULDN'T BELIEVE her ears.

Had Lord Archer truly said what she thought he'd said? *Yes.* But...

Why?

Why was she to meet Lord Nestor?

In a world of bad ideas, it was the worst.

But the sound in Lord Archer's voice said it all.

While she might be on the point of apoplexy, he was enjoying himself.

"Meet the contessa?" asked Lord Nestor. "Why would I need

to do that?"

See? She wasn't the only one who thought the idea terrible.

"She's quite mystical about it, really," said Lord Archer, grave.

Mystical? Truly, the man was astounding.

"She says she'll know when she has met the Arabian's true soul owner."

What nonsense was this?

Valentina risked a glance toward Lord Nestor. The man looked utterly flummoxed. *"Soul owner?"* He snorted. *"Women."*

Lord Archer lifted his hands in a gesture of helplessness. "She's already met Kilmuir. I think she quite liked him."

"Kilmuir?" burst from Lord Nestor's mouth. "That Scottish brute? What does he have to do with this?"

Lord Archer shrugged an indifferent shoulder. "Says he might be interested."

"What does Kilmuir know about horseflesh?" Lord Nestor didn't give Lord Archer the chance reply. "When can I meet her?"

Lord Archer's gaze screwed up to the sky, as if searching for the answer there. Valentina's every last nerve frazzled to the end, and he looked as cool as a light spring breeze.

And it struck her.

Lord Archer was in his element.

Valentina, on the other hand, preferred that the rules be laid out clearly, and that everyone play by them. Black and white, no gray space.

The gray was where Lord Archer thrived and frolicked.

"The contessa has expressed an interest in a visit to Hyde Park on the morrow."

"Name the time," said Lord Nestor.

The more intense Lord Nestor became, the more relaxed Lord Archer appeared. But Valentina guessed his heart was racing just as fast as hers. Not from fright, like hers, but from pure excitement. "Eight of the clock."

"That's rather late for a Hyde Park visit."

"In the morning."

"I never rise before ten."

Lord Archer shrugged. "Perhaps tomorrow you will. The contessa rises with the sun."

It was all Valentina could do not to snort. She'd never risen with the sun in all her life. The only time she'd ever seen a sunrise was this very morning with this blasted, frustrating man.

"Fine," said Lord Nestor. He looked none too pleased about it.

Well, it appeared she and Lord Nestor shared something in common.

"Remember to be at your most charming." Lord Archer couldn't resist toying with his quarry, like a cat.

"At eight in the morning?" Lord Nestor snorted. "Not bloody likely."

"And don't forget a gift."

"What does the chit like?" Lord Nestor was getting grumpy and petulant like a fractious child pushed too far.

But Lord Archer wouldn't—or *couldn't*, more like—stop. He was having too much fun. "Small, furry animals."

Valentina squeaked a surprised, "Yip!" then coughed to cover it up.

Lord Nestor peered around so as to get a good look at her, and Valentina ducked her head so all he could see was the top of her floppy hat.

Earlier, when she'd arrived in the receiving hall dressed as a stable lad, Lord Archer had taken one look at her and said, "You'll have to batten those down."

She'd immediately gone hot. "What do you mean?"

But she'd known what he meant. *Her breasts.* It wasn't enough to dress in men's clothing and tie one's hair back in a queue. One's breasts couldn't be swinging all willy-nilly beneath one's shirt.

"And take this." He'd thrust a big, floppy hat in her direction.

Within the large, terrible idea of the ruse they were attempting to perpetrate, it had been a good idea, she could see now as she took refuge behind it.

"Is your stable lad unwell?" asked Lord Nestor.

"He squeaks like that when he needs to be oiled," said Lord Archer without a hint of humor.

Valentina poked her head up just enough to catch Lord Nestor's reaction. He was looking at Lord Archer as if he'd sprouted another head. "A small, furry animal?" he asked, continuing their conversation.

"Oh, you know, like a puppy or a kitten or a vole or a mole, for that matter."

"Right," said Lord Nestor, slowly. The man looked ready to bolt.

Lord Archer must have drawn the same conclusion as Valentina—that perhaps he'd pushed a step past the edge—for he directed a small bow toward Lord Nestor and said, "Until tomorrow."

He pivoted on his heel and vacated the stable at an uncomfortably fast clip. Valentina struggled to draw abreast with him. She had a few words to say to this man. More than a few, in fact.

"Not yet," he muttered. "We'll talk when we're in the hackney."

Of course, it took several minutes to wade through all the greetings that came Lord Archer's way—the man was truly popular—and hail a hackney cab. Once inside, they sat opposite each other.

Heavens, but the man was attractive. His hair that had caught the sun and kept it. His face that had been chiseled from stone. His long, lanky form that somehow spoke of both strength and elegance. In combination with that personality of his, he was too much.

This wasn't a good time to have those thoughts.

Not that there would ever be a good time.

"You'll have me meet Lord Nestor?" she asked, the question emerging as an accusation. "As a *contessa*?" It all defied belief, but particularly that last part.

His smile widened. "Isn't it perfect?"

He would think that.

"Perfect? For whom?"

"Did you see the way Nestor took the bait?"

Was the man impervious to the obvious? "How am I to impersonate a contessa?" She started with the most obvious. "I have nothing to wear."

He waved the fact away as mere detail. "You can borrow a riding habit from Delilah."

"That won't work."

"Then from Juliet."

"That won't work either."

His gaze narrowed on Valentina. "One would think you don't wish this entire plan to work."

Valentina pointed out the obvious. "Your sister and cousin stand a good six inches taller than me, for starters."

"Tucker will take care of it."

She canted her head. "Nothing is impossible in your world, is it?"

"Should it be?" The man had the temerity to look flummoxed. Then the mischief returned to his eye. "We have Nestor all but caught, but it would be good to string him along for a while. We can't make it too easy."

"Why not?" she asked, exasperated. "I think he would hand over the money today."

Lord Archer shook his head. "He needs to work for it a bit longer. Justice isn't so easily served." His gaze narrowed on Valentina. She shifted uncomfortably in her seat. "*You* must make him work for it."

She exhaled a gusty, frustrated breath. He looked utterly unbothered. People must have directed gusty, frustrated breaths in his direction every day of his life. "Why make it difficult?"

"Haven't you noticed? People like a little difficulty. If it simply falls into Nestor's lap, he'll grow suspicious. The man might be greedy, but he's not entirely stupid. Leave it to me. Not only will your family and the others get their money, they'll get a heap of justice, too."

She didn't know why she should believe this barmy lord she'd known for fewer than four and twenty hours, but she did.

Still, there was something she needed to say. "I think they would be satisfied simply with the money."

"Ah, but I wouldn't."

And there it was, peeking through his glib words and smile. The depth she'd sensed in him. He wasn't only a barmy lord, was he?

He rubbed his hands together. "Now we pull a swindle on the swindler." He thought for a second. "A double swindle, if you will." Another second of thought. "The swindler becomes the swindled."

She laughed. She couldn't help herself. "You really like saying that word."

"It does possess a certain panache."

Like the man who spoke it.

Soon, they reached Casa Windermere, as Lord Archer called it. Detached from its neighbors, it was a truly spectacular mansion, all red brick and towering white columns and clean lines and imposing elegance. As she stepped inside, she became suddenly awkward. The possessor of all *this* was helping her. "I'll just change out of these clothes now."

"We'll see you at the evening meal?"

She gave a noncommittal nod and made her way toward her room. Once inside, she closed the door and exhaled slowly.

A surprising thought came to her.

She was relieved that Lord Archer was a friend, and not an enemy.

For all his light and charm, something deeper resided within him. A relentlessness. And something else, too... Something more substantive than the blithe façade he presented. Something solid inside him.

It intrigued and pulled her in, though she knew she should resist.

For that look in his eyes—emanating from the part of him that was *deeper*—called to a *deeper* part of herself.

A part that longed to respond.

Chapter Six

Night

A<small>T FIRST,</small> V<small>ALENTINA</small> resisted opening her eyes. She was so very tired, and this bed was so very comfortable.

But music that held a vague familiarity kept wafting through her dreams on light, buoyant notes…

The piano music from yesterday. The music Lord Archer said had come from a neighboring manse.

Her eyes fluttered open, and her ears strained toward the sound.

This music… It was coming from within this manse.

On instinct, she swept the covers aside and hopped to the floor, feet landing on plush Persian wool. She grabbed a night-rail and cinched it tightly about her waist.

Lady Delilah and Miss Windermere had sent her a variety of clothing that was all exactly six inches too long for her, as she'd predicted. Tucker had her work cut out for her. Still, Valentina was appreciative. Their intentions were in the right place, which seemed to be a Windermere family trait.

Night-rail trailing on the floor behind her, Valentina let the music guide her out of her room. She hadn't any idea where she was going, but she didn't need to know. All she need do was follow the haunting notes through the moonlit mansion. Across the corridor…down the wide staircase…across another corridor… The music pulled her along as though she hadn't a choice but to follow it. In the still slate gray of night, only she and it existed.

She came to a closed door framed in a rim of soft golden light. She pressed her ear to solid wood and listened, feeling each lush note vibrate through her. She shouldn't twist the handle and open the door. She understood that. She hadn't been invited.

But a feeling tugged at her. She *needed* to open the door, and it had everything to do with the lie Lord Archer had told her yesterday, and the suspicion that pulled at her tonight. The music was *here*—in this house. So, why hadn't he told her the truth?

She cracked the door open and poked her head inside. In the half light of the hearth's low fire stretched a gentleman's study, all rich woods and mahogany leather, a vast stretch of floor-to-ceiling bookcases on this wall, a massive map of the world on that one. But her eyes only caught those characteristics in periphery, for they immediately flew toward the source of the music in the farthest corner.

There, bent over the piano keyboard before a bow window, sat Lord Archer.

Her instinct was confirmed.

His back to her, entirely concentrated on the music pouring from the instrument, he hadn't heard her enter. He wore nothing but a white linen shirt and trousers, his feet bare, shirtsleeves rolled to his elbows.

And his hands... his large, skilled hands commanded the black and white keys—imploring them, enticing them, provoking them—leaving them no choice but to bend to his will.

Valentina kept to the periphery of the room so he wouldn't notice her. She didn't want him to stop for anything. The music flowing from his fingertips was weaving a night spell around her.

Yet she kept moving. She needed to see his face.

But it was his chest she first noticed, with his shirt flopped open in a V, offering an unexpected view of muscles and golden hair that led downward... He was a gorgeous man. It had to be a fact universally acknowledged. But his utter absorption in his playing… That was unexpected. He appeared utterly unlike himself.

Or more correctly, utterly unlike the Lord Archer she'd come to know.

Or thought she'd known.

Intense…emotional…wrecked.

His fingers stopped on a wild flourish. The last note echoed through the room before going dead silent. He raked a hand through tousled curls. Frustration radiated off him in all but visible waves.

"That was—"

His head whipped up, and intense blue eyes bored into her.

Who was this man? Surely not Lord Archer.

Could he have a twin?

"What are you doing here?" he snapped.

"I…I…" she stammered. Then she realized she didn't need to find an excuse to be here. The truth would do. "I followed the music. It's magical."

Gaze unflinching, Lord Archer let a snort speak for him.

She noticed a pencil behind his ear and large pieces of composition paper scattered about the fallboard. Another suspicion nipped at her. "Whose composition were you playing?"

"No one worth noting," he near growled.

There. She had it. *Confirmation.*

"It's haunting"—she took a step—"and beautiful"—another step—"and—"

"Hardly," he muttered.

She reached the piano and tapped a sheet of composition paper. "It's *yours.*"

"Does an artist truly ever own one's work?"

"Lord Archer—"

"Not just a pretty face, are you?"

"I've been told I have a pretty voice, too," she said. It was always best to give as one got with this man.

"That you do."

She was so close she could smell his scent of cloves, spice, and man. So close she could reach out and touch him. One act involuntary, the other...requiring agency. "Play me the rest of it," she demanded.

He blew a frustrated raspberry. "There is no *rest of it*."

Ah.

"You're stuck."

"You needn't sound so pleased," he said, pettish.

A laugh escaped her. "It's simply a relief to know you're not perfect, Lord Archer."

His head cocked, and he regarded her with a quizzical expression. "Perfect? Me?" A dry, humorless laugh sounded through his nose. "You clearly have me mistaken for someone else."

This sudden turn of conversation struck Valentina sideways.

To all outward appearances, the man before her epitomized the world's opinion on male perfection. Wealth, title, dashing good looks, charming smile, confidence in everything he did.

But looking into his eyes now, it occurred to her that he might not see himself in that light at all. Before her was none of that blithe, devil-may-care confidence—a façade he presented to the world, she was beginning to understand.

Instead, she saw those depths she'd noted yesterday.

She saw an artist tortured by his work.

She saw a Lord Archer who not only intrigued her, but pulled at her.

Shockingly, this Lord Archer was someone she wanted to know better.

For she suspected she hadn't known him at all until this very moment.

※

ARCHIE WASN'T CERTAIN what irritated him more.

That Miss Hart had invaded his private sanctuary, uninvited—after all, every member of the household from sister to scullery maid knew to stay away when he sat at the piano.

Or that she'd invaded his private sanctuary looking like original sin itself—sable hair sleep-tousled and tumbling to her waist in soft waves; night-rail cinched but not so tightly that a hint of voluptuous cleavage wasn't offered; her lips, ruby-red and lush and practically begging for a kiss…

That last bit had nothing to do with sleep, but more to do with the original sin part.

The woman was a temptation.

And she seemed to have no idea.

"Will you play the piece from the beginning?" she asked.

"You don't have to ask."

"Pardon?"

"To be polite."

Her lips curled into a smile. "I wouldn't. There is too much terrible music in the world to willingly subject oneself to it."

He should tell her to leave. His music was his alone. He was simply a gentleman musician hobbyist.

And that was all he would ever be. Yet…

He wanted to play for her.

She continued. "What you were playing just now…"

"Yes?" Every muscle in his body tensed in anticipation of her answer.

"Your music isn't that." Her direct gaze held his, left him no room for charm or glibness.

"Isn't what?"

"Terrible."

"Well, that's something, at least."

She smoothed her palm across the sheets of music spread across the fallboard. "Shall I turn the pages for you?"

He shook his head. "I don't need them."

His fingers hovered above the keyboard. He didn't have to do this. He was in no way obligated to play for her.

Except he wanted to.

And obligations and desires were two different entities entirely.

With banked intention, softly, his fingers came down on the keys. One note, then another, followed by a chord, then another, as the notes flowed from him, his fingertips becoming an extension of his soul, as they always did when he sat down to his instrument. His body swaying with the motion of his hands, he poured his entire being into the piece, fully succumbing to the music—*his* music—for his audience of one.

Her head tipped slightly to the side and eyes half closed, her entire being appeared concentrated in the act of listening.

His playing slowed. He was nearing the end of the piece. Well, not the end, but all he had.

Her eyes opened and met his. Knowledge shone within. She'd noticed the music losing its momentum, losing what magic it had possessed in the beginning.

She held up a hand, palm extended out. She was asking, nay, telling him to stop. *"There,"* she said.

"There where?"

"Play it again," she said. "This time more slowly."

Annoyed, Archie started from the beginning. *Slowly*, as commanded. Her gaze drifted away and into the distance, her head canted to the side. Her forefinger shot into the air, and her entire face went bright. *"There!"*

This again?

"There *where?*" he demanded.

"Don't you hear it after the C sharp?"

"Hear what precisely?" In some small way, he wanted to hear her opinion. But in a larger way, he didn't. They always said artists were ticklish. He was no different.

"You take it into the major scale from there—"

"Yes," he said slowly.

"And then you give yourself nowhere interesting to go."

Archie blinked. No one wanted to hear their artistic endeavor almost called...*boring*. But he half suspected she might be saying exactly that. It was quite possibly the first time in his life anyone had almost called him boring.

She spread her hands wide and apologetic. "You've written yourself into a corner."

As she began humming, his fingers intuitively began playing, in perfect synch with the road she was leading him down. "So you're suggesting I take it…" He let his fingers do the rest of his talking.

She nodded. "Into the minor scale."

And like that, the piece opened up, and fresh vistas spread before him, even as the emotion of the music deepened and took on an unexpected complexity.

A feeling took wing inside him and soared. This specific feeling—of creation, of freedom—the promise of it was what pushed him out of bed in the mornings. It was what he lived for. If happiness had a purified form, it lay here. If he could bottle it, he could sell it for the price of diamonds.

He lifted his hands off the keys and shot to his feet, reaching for the pencil behind his ear. Line by line, the notes flew from his mind and onto paper. He saw the piece clearly to the end now, and understood it was his best work yet.

And it was thanks to the woman standing by his side—his muse—watching quietly and nodding every so often while he transcribed her suggestions. The dark mood that had hung over his work these last several months lifted, and light entered his soul. The transformation was no more or less dramatic than that.

Some five minutes—or fifty minutes—later, he straightened. It was done. What relief lay within that simple sentence. He met Miss Hart's gaze with a smile. He might never stop smiling. "I could kiss you," he said, without thinking.

Miss Hart blushed, and her gaze skittered away. "I'm sure there's no need for that."

Archie's brow gathered. Of a sudden, he wanted to kiss her. A simple kiss of gratitude, really.

He leaned over and bussed a quick peck on her cheek.

She laughed. He did, too.

"And if we do it like the Italians..." He leaned in and kissed her other cheek.

But he made a mistake with the second kiss.

He inhaled.

And allowed his senses to fill with her. *Lemon...roses...Valentina...*

And when she laughed this time, knowledge entered her eyes.

And when he leaned in again, she didn't shy away. She let him press his mouth against her lush, ruby-red, made-for-sin lips. In fact, she might have leaned in a little herself. Then she exhaled a light sigh into his mouth.

Her arms reached around his neck, her fingernails lightly grazing along the nape, sending shivers up his spine, at the same moment his hand cupped the back of her head and the other found the small of her back. Shorter than him by a good ten inches, her body strained up the length of his, and the kiss deepened as he turned her around so her back pressed against the piano. His cock, hard and ready, pushed against her belly, and guided by instinct rather than experience, her hips gave a swivel.

Oh, Lord.

He could have her here...*now*...against the piano. That was what the swivel of her hips and urgent whimpers of desire were telling him.

In truth, it had always been a fantasy of his—to tup a woman silly against a piano.

But with Valentina... It would be no mere tupping.

On a wave of noble determination and self-denial, he removed his hands from her body and stepped away. Separated by mere inches, they stared at each other, gasping for air. She was deliciously tousled, her lips puffy and kiss-crushed—a fantasy come to life.

He took another step back.

For her.

For himself.

"I, um…" She touched fingertips to those lips in need of more thorough kissing. "I need to go to bed."

"Alone?" he asked.

Oh, what wasn't wrong about that question? Yet…

He waited with held breath for her answer.

She nodded, once. "Alone."

Of course, alone.

He could be a dolt. It was a fact.

She clasped her night-rail tightly to her neck—he could tell her it was too late for such modesty, but decided to leave it unsaid—and whirled around, exiting the room in short fashion, leaving Archie, indeed, alone.

With his thoughts and misdeeds.

For that kiss had, indeed, been a misdeed.

He must rein himself in. That was clear.

He was to help Miss Hart—*not* help himself *to* her. He must keep reminding himself.

Not so fine a distinction as the language would suggest.

Yet the kiss confirmed what he'd already suspected. Something beyond the musical pulsed between them.

Attraction…desire…

It wasn't so much that it had been awakened just now, as expressed.

He didn't have much practice curbing his desires.

Yet for the sake of his music and his muse he must try.

Chapter Seven

Next day

VALENTINA TOOK THE first step down the wide, magnificent staircase of Casa Windermere, wearing a peacock-blue, borrowed-and-hemmed riding habit, and resisted the urge to turn tail and run.

After all, the Windermere brood standing at the base of the stairs hadn't yet noticed her. They were too busy loudly debating some topic or another. There was always a topic up for debate in this household.

She'd never worn clothing so fine, or so fitted. It would seem this riding habit had come from the closet of Miss Windermere, who, while taller than Valentina, was about the same size everywhere else. Except for one area. The bosom. Between the tightly laced stays and the fifty or so buttons up the bodice, her breasts had nowhere to go but up—nearly to her chin. They were making quite a spectacle of themselves.

The scales were tipping heavily toward tucking her skirts into her drawers and seeing how fast she could leg it, when Lady Delilah's eyes swung up, and the rest followed, and it was entirely too late for Valentina. She was trapped.

Continuing her descent, she attempted to keep her gaze averted from Archie, feeling sheepish and unready after last night's kiss.

Now that she knew the taste of his lips that was how she

thought of him. *Archie.*

But her attempt failed. She had to know how he would look in the full light of day.

It turned out he looked exactly like his usual self—not at all like his night self. Dressed in riding clothes and lightly slapping a crop against his muscled thigh, his day self was as handsome as his night self.

He flicked a quick glance her way, but his gaze didn't linger. She could almost convince herself last night had been a dream.

If her lips weren't still tingling from his kiss.

"Well, that's a relief," he said to Lady Delilah.

"What are you speaking of, dear brother?" asked Lady Delilah, mischief in her eyes.

"I thought it fully possible you would cause some mischief and lend Miss Hart a nun's habit," he said. "You're contrary that way. No use denying it."

"Why would I deny it?" she asked. "It's one of my defining characteristics. But you're likely correct. Nestor wouldn't take to a prudish sort of contessa, but rather the obvious sort."

Valentina bristled with sudden umbrage. "Are you saying I'm an obvious sort of woman?"

Lady Delilah—in fact, all three sets of eyes—gave her a quick up-and-down once-over. "Don't take this the wrong way," said Lady Delilah, hands spread wide in a gesture of helplessness. "But, yes."

One, then two, heavy beats of time ticked past as everyone waited for Valentina's reaction.

It was Miss Windermere who broke the silence. "In the loveliest way, of course."

Valentina couldn't decide if she'd been insulted or complimented.

Archie gave his thigh another slap with the riding crop. "Right."

Valentina kept searching for the slightest hint of last night in his eyes, but found nothing. Perhaps it *had* been a dream...

"Now we ride on to Rotten Row," he said, moving toward the door along with his siblings.

Valentina hadn't been looking forward to this moment, but there was no more avoiding it. Her feet remained planted, and she cleared her throat. "There's a problem."

One by one they pivoted to get a look at her. It was Archie who asked, "What's that?"

She would have to put it bluntly. "I've never set bottom on a horse in all my life."

Stunned silence followed. Lady Delilah broke it with her laugh. "Oh, this is too delicious."

Archie's dark blond eyebrows collided in the middle of his forehead. He looked utterly flummoxed, as if her confession refused to harmonize with his view of the world. "Everyone rides, don't they?"

"No," said Valentina, firm, definite.

"Right," he said slowly.

"Well, then you'll just need a quick lesson," said Miss Windermere with an encouraging smile.

That seemed to rally Archie. "Of course, a quick lesson." He swung the front door open and waved at Valentina to follow him. "You have ten minutes to become a skilled horsewoman, *Contessa*."

Ten minutes later

VALENTINA HAD MANAGED to climb onto the horse's back.

And stay there.

That was something.

For now.

Reins clutched to her chest for dear life, a thin sheen of perspiration coating her body, she kept her gaze fastened onto Archie's back, as Lady Delilah and Miss Windermere rode to her rear.

"If she comes unhorsed," Lady Delilah had said, "Juliet and I can scoop her up."

Not exactly words of reassurance.

Seated on a sidesaddle, and even with one knee hooked over the pommel, Valentina's position felt precarious and unbalanced. All she wanted to do was set feet on dear terra firma again.

Who had devised this mode of riding for women, anyway? It would be far better if she rode with the sort of saddle that allowed her to straddle the horse. But, oh no, that simply wasn't *done*. Archie had laughed as he'd made that last point. Apparently, she would look like the world's biggest hoyden straddling a horse in Hyde Park.

Every clip-clop of the horse's hooves rattled her teeth inside her head. While, just ahead, Archie rode ever so smoothly, as if he'd been born in the saddle. She snorted. Mayhap he had been. She was learning that the lives of aristocrats were as eccentric as the gossip rags made them out to be.

Countess Gives Birth in the Saddle.

The headline wouldn't shock Valentina one bit.

For now, however, she had more practical realities to consider for Archie had urged his mount into a trot. How was she to keep pace? Fortunately, or unfortunately for her rump, her horse seemed to have an idea as it fell into step behind him, leaving her no choice but to notice things about him.

Like, how attractive he was with his hair glinting gold in the morning sun. And how broad his shoulders appeared in his impeccably cut riding coat. And the way his body moved with utter command and a certain looseness as they rode across London streets that were now waking to the day ahead.

At last—though it couldn't have been more than ten minutes—they reached the verdant environs of Hyde Park. Archie slowed his mount to a walk and drew abreast with her. "You truly are a terrible rider, Miss Hart," he said. "I've never witnessed anyone less suited to a horse. Can't you simply relax into the ride?"

"No." It was that simple.

His mouth widened into his too-charming smile. "Aw, but Miss Muffet is truly a sweet, old girl," he said, reaching over to stroke the mare's mane.

Valentina had a very different relationship with sweet, old Miss Muffet. "She nipped at me." She still felt sour about it.

Archie shrugged. "Well, that's down to you. You really should have brought her a sweet."

The cheek of the man! "I know nothing of horses."

Again, he shrugged. "Now you do. Anyway, it's a good thing you're so good-looking. Perhaps Nestor won't notice that you don't know one end of a horse from the other."

Even as she considered defending herself from such slander, her mouth snapped shut.

A sliver of heat from his suddenly intense gaze cut through her—to a place deep and dark and interior. It stole her breath away; that heat, from this man.

To incite and capture the heat of a man like Lord Archer—a man who appeared to sail through life with blithe cool—it felt strangely special.

Then he shifted his gaze and fixed his mouth into the smile she'd come to know. He leaned in her direction. "We're on."

She followed his gaze. There, twenty yards ahead, was Lord Nestor riding toward them. Disgust surged through Valentina. Here was the man who'd decided it was his lordly prerogative to take what he wanted and ruin good men and families in the process. He was vile, and though she had her doubts about Archie's methods, Valentina was suddenly grateful for his involvement in securing her family's savings.

"Nestor, old chap," Archie called. "You made it out."

"You're the one who's late, Archer," groused Nestor.

Lady Delilah laughed. "We Windermeres tend to have a loose association with timekeeping."

"In short, we don't have any use for it," said Archie unapologetically.

Nestor's gaze settled on Valentina. His eyebrows drew together quizzically. He was probably wondering why this Italian contessa, who he'd never met, was scowling at him. She made an attempt to relax her face and offer a smile.

Her lips lifted a fraction.

This approximation of a smile would have to do.

"Greetings, Contessa," he said with a tip of his hat.

Valentina opened her mouth to reply, when Archie jumped in, "Poor thing doesn't speak a lick of English."

Her mouth snapped shut. Even as irritation streaked through her, she saw the wisdom of the choice. Nestor would know her for a low-born country bumpkin the instant she spoke her first hello.

And that would be good-bye.

Nestor shrugged indifferently and cast his gaze about. "Where's the Arabian?"

All charm, Lord Nestor.

"Oh, I convinced the contessa not to bring him up to Town."

Nestor's mouth turned down at the edges. It seemed to have found its customary position. "Smart of you, Archer," he said a bit meanly. He was the sort of man who needed to make everyone who happened across his path feel inferior so he could feel superior. *Vile.*

Archie leaned in conspiratorially. "We wouldn't be able to contain the hordes of gentlemen clamoring to get a look. No, the Arabian is being transported to Epsom Downs as we speak."

Nestor nodded slowly, the wheels of his mind turning for all to see. A skepticism hung about him this morning that hadn't been there yesterday when he'd been in the fresh throes of greed. Perhaps overnight, the idea had occurred to him that Lord Archer might be playing him for a fool.

The very idea set Valentina's nerves on edge, because, well, he'd be absolutely correct. Lord Archer was, indeed, playing him for a fool.

And all for a lark.

But to look at him, one would never know it, for he showed no sign of nerves. Valentina wanted to run her fingertips over his palm, just to see if she found a slick of sweat. She suspected she wouldn't.

"Just look at her, old chap," said Archie.

It only occurred to Valentina that the *her* in question was...*her*.

All eyes were suddenly upon her. She tried not to squirm, mostly so as not to give Miss Muffet any ideas of bolting.

"I'm not sure she's feeling all that great about your spirit," he continued.

Lord Nestor's face darkened, and his eyes narrowed on her. Valentina's heart kicked into a sprint, but she saw what Archie had done. He'd sensed Nestor's misgiving and turned it around on him.

Of a sudden, Lady Delilah opened her mouth and began spewing rapid Italian at Valentina. She recognized one of every four words, in particular the word *fugazi*. It seemed Lady Delilah, with a broad, blameless smile on her face, was calling Lord *Fester* a fake to his face. Valentina nodded and inserted the odd, "Mm-hmm."

These Windermeres were unequal to nothing.

Once Lady Delilah finished her thorough dressing down of Lord Nestor, which he accepted with a blank stare, Archie's head cocked. "Nestor, I do believe your pocket just meowed."

Valentina braced herself. She'd forgotten the promise of a small, furry gift.

On a sigh, Lord Nestor opened his riding coat and dug into an inner pocket. "Ouch!" His hand recoiled to reveal an alarming amount of blood on the tip of his thumb.

Archie flashed Valentina a quick glance. Equal parts of amusement and alarm shone in his eyes. Then the man winked.

She should be annoyed, really she should, but instead, she found herself biting back a smile. This was serious business, his wink seemed to say, but why couldn't serious business be fun, too?

The view of the world he offered was unlike any she'd ever encountered, and she thought she might like it.

She might even like *him*.

Chapter Eight

"**Y**OU DIDN'T BRING the contessa a serpent, did you?" asked Archie.

Nestor would be the sort to take a serpent for a soft, cuddly pet.

Nestor tried again, this time his hand emerging from the interior pocket with a hissing gray ball of fur. Wide, milky blue eyes flying frantically about, the kitten showed its tiny, sharp teeth. This kitten meant business.

Nestor thrust the animal toward Valentina. With a faltering smile that didn't reach her eyes, she accepted the little beast gingerly, *ooo*ing and *ahh*ing and pretending to be delighted. One could only thank the heavens for kidskin gloves, though Valentina's would be tatters by the time they returned home. Really, though, the kitten was adorable with its little, pushed-in face, even if it wouldn't stop hissing.

Valentina flicked Archie a thoroughly irritated glance. Barely able to suppress the laugh that wanted out, he couldn't have asked for this morning to go any better. Valentina, however, didn't appear to share his optimism as she held the kitten safely away from her.

The air picked up the sound of hooves thundering in the distance. Archie pivoted in the saddle to find Rory riding toward them. Right on time. First thing this morning, Archie had sent his friend a note, asking him to meet them in Hyde Park. He'd figured after a night to think it over, Nestor might have some doubts. A little competition should bring him back in line.

Valentina's question from yesterday nagged at him. Why was he dragging this out?

Justice, yes. In the end, Valentina's family would get theirs, and Nestor would get his. A tidy outcome.

But that wasn't the only reason why.

That woman, who sat her horse badly and was presently wrestling a tiny kitten who might be winning, was inspiration. Last night, at the piano… He hadn't felt that inspired in years.

And the kiss…

It had inspired, too.

His gaze settled on her mouth. It couldn't help itself.

He shouldn't kiss that mouth again.

Truly, what had he been thinking?

It wasn't that he didn't kiss women. He'd, in fact, kissed quite a few.

But he didn't kiss virtuous women.

Not women like Valentina.

Right.

"Nestor, I believe you're acquainted with Lord Kilmuir?"

Nestor nodded, curt. Rory gave the same back. Archie cleared his throat. Now was the time for Rory to speak his line. The one that would light a fire beneath Nestor.

Rory snapped to. "The Arabian," burst from him. "Is it here?"

He might rival Valentina with his acting skills.

Nestor sat taller in his saddle. "What is this?"

"I don't really see the harm in cutting Kilmuir in," said Archie easily.

Nestor shook his head. He wasn't having it. "Just you and me, Archer. No Kilmuir."

Archie lifted his hands in a gesture of helplessness, and Rory's chest puffed out in indignation. "What fresh perfidy is this?" he bellowed.

Archie had to keep from rolling his eyes. Delilah and Juliet were stifling snickers behind him. But, really, Rory was laying it on a bit thick. Nestor didn't seem to notice. "There's only room for two investors in this deal, Kilmuir. Find yourself another horse."

Archie shrugged, as if helpless. "You heard the man."

Rory lifted a hand into the air and shouted, "This shall not be the last ye've heard of me!" And he charged away on his mount.

Archie resisted the urge to clap for his friend's performance. But truly, when one involved a man's ego, what swindles couldn't be perpetrated? Had he not been born a lord, he'd have enjoyed a satisfying career in the hustling of aristocrats.

"Tomorrow night," said Archie. It was time to bring the meeting to a conclusion. He'd gotten what he wanted out of it.

"What is tomorrow night?" asked Nestor. He'd begun watching Valentina carefully. Too carefully.

"You'll have your answer at my sister Amelia's musicale tomorrow night." An invitation to the Duke and Duchess of Ripon's soirée was one of the most highly sought-after invitations in Town.

And Archie knew Nestor wouldn't have received one.

Nestor cleared his throat, embarrassed. "I'm afraid I shall not be attending."

Archie waved a dismissive hand. "Oh, your invitation must've been lost in the post. I'll have my sister send another by messenger today."

Archie sensed a subtle puffing of the other man's chest. He'd just given Nestor what he truly wanted—a road back into the top tier of society after all the scandals of his family.

Archie hoped Nestor enjoyed the trip. It would be a short one.

Archie went suddenly serious. "And be on the lookout for The Nod."

"The Nod?"

"If she gives me The Nod tomorrow night, you're in."

Again, Nestor's gaze settled on Valentina, and his eyes narrowed. Archie understood what had caught Nestor's attention. Valentina was having a devil of a time settling the kitten, and every time she moved she overcorrected. In the last thirty seconds, the woman had nearly unhorsed herself twice.

"Why is the contessa such a poor horsewoman?" asked Nestor, an understatement of the obvious. "I've never seen a lady sit a horse at such an awkward angle."

"I've learned to never question the Italian way," said Archie. "Besides, she has a bad bottom."

A choking sound erupted from Valentina. Archie didn't dare look. "Some sort of woman issue," he finished on a shrug. It was all that ever needed to be said to relieve a man of his curiosity regarding the opposite sex. *Woman issue.*

"Oh!" Valentina exclaimed. She looked poised to say more when Delilah cut in and began firing Italian at her.

Archie glanced over in time to watch the kitten's tail disappear beneath Miss Muffet's mane. The kitten had escaped. It was definitely time to conclude this meeting, for Archie sensed havoc careening their way. He had a nose for it.

Then all hell broke loose. The horse sprang forward on a lurch and set off across the grass, racing away with Valentina hanging on for dear life. The kitten's razor-sharp claws must have dug beneath Miss Muffet's fur and found skin.

Oh, Lord.

"It's a race!" Archie called over his shoulder as he gave chase.

Of course, it wasn't a race, but Valentina needed saving as Miss Muffet was making straight for the Serpentine. Surely, she would stop before—

And Miss Muffet did stop before reaching the water.

By about a foot.

Momentum lifted Valentina off her sidesaddle and into the air, causing her to launch over Miss Muffet's head and land directly on her tuffet, before sinking. Archie's horse was still in motion as he dismounted and jumped into the river after her. The water, however, wasn't very deep, and Valentina was standing by the time he reached her.

"Are you harmed?" he asked, only resisting taking her in his arms to check for himself.

She'd transformed into a sopping wet, sputtering mess of a woman, clumps of hair and pond muck streaming down her face, her hands held away from her body. He met disbelief and perplexity in wide, unblinking eyes.

On the riverbank, Miss Muffet whinnied, and between her ears poked a furry, little gray face, milky blue eyes glaring down at them. "Meow."

A long beat of time stretched before Archie and Valentina burst into laughter at the exact same instant.

Nestor reined in his horse well away from the riverbank, watching them as if they'd lost what few wits they'd possessed in the first place.

"Join us?" asked Archie. "It's an Italian custom when deals are being made."

Nestor's eyebrows lifted in disbelief. "To jump into a river?"

"Julius Caesar refused and look where that got him," said Archie.

Nestor gave his head a slow shake. "I'll see you at the Duke and Duchess of Ripon's musicale tomorrow, Archer."

And with that, Nestor was gone.

Good riddance.

Archie glanced over to find Valentina scowling at him. "What have I done wrong?" No use beating around the bush.

"Julius Caesar was Italian," she stated. She would look quite formidable if it weren't for the long, thin blade of pond grass hanging from her chin, giving her, quite frankly, the appearance of a billy goat.

"And?"

"You must stop speaking of Italians as if they are naught but brainless buffoons."

"Of course, I don't believe that," said Archie. "But English society thinks anyone not them is a savage. I'm simply playing to Nestor's preconceived notions."

"Well, stop," she blasted at him. "My mother is Italian, and she's the most intelligent and reasonable woman I've ever known." She exhaled a frustrated sigh. "The Italians gave the world the Renaissance. They gave the world culture when the only people populating this island of yours were, indeed, savages."

A rare sheepishness overcame Archie. She was in the right. "I sincerely apologize, Miss Hart. It was wrongly done of me."

Her gaze searched his, and at last, she nodded her acceptance of his apology. His spirits lifted.

He clambered up the riverbank, then turned and held out his hand to her. She hesitated. She was still annoyed with him, and rightfully so. But with her wool riding habit thoroughly soaked, she needed his help. Finally, she took his hand, and he gave a great heave, pulling her onto dry land.

Panting with the combined effort, they stood not six inches apart. Her hand, cold and wet, remained in his, but her cheeks were bright and flushed. And in her eyes shone something other than annoyance.

Knowledge.

Knowledge that only existed between them.

Knowledge of last night.

"If it isn't the family Windermere!" came a voice from the not-too-far distance.

Valentina snatched her hand back and stepped away from Archie. He felt the loss, even as he understood its necessity.

Delilah groaned, and Juliet giggled.

Approaching them with his too-high top hat and solid brass cane was none other than the tall, sharpishly thin figure of Mr. Oliver Quincy, the man who two years ago had fallen in love with Delilah at first sight and proposed marriage at second during a social assembly in the village of Bumpstead Hollow. Delilah had laughed for a solid minute before soundly rejecting him. Quincy, however, hadn't been in the least embarrassed. He hadn't enough sense to experience embarrassment.

"What have we here?" the man asked, taking in their motley little grouping.

"A trifling mishap is all," said Archie. He'd noticed that Valentina had begun shivering. "She needs something warm and dry," he said to anyone who would listen. His own overcoat was soaked.

Quincy didn't take the hint. It was Delilah who played gallant as she shed her spencer and handed it down to Valentina.

"Archie," said Juliet, "help her up onto my saddle. She can ride home with me."

"Um," began Valentina, clearly adding up the steps it would take to get her off the ground and onto Juliet's mount.

Archie met Valentina's eye. "Nothing to it."

Still, she didn't move.

"Trust me," he said, only to her.

She swallowed before finally surrendering to the idea. She must've reached the conclusion that she was outnumbered by Windermeres. Resistance would be futile.

"Where do you want me?" she asked, and instantly froze.

Given last night's kiss, it was a question laden with possibility. *No.*

"Erm," began Archie, attempting to correct the direction of his thoughts. "Stand here." He indicated a place at the side of the horse. Once she'd done as instructed, he continued, "Now, when I say hop, you jump with all your might."

Wary eyebrows crinkled together.

He stepped forward and placed his hands on her waist.

"What—"

"It's necessary."

Her waist was tiny. Her presence loomed so large for him that he could forget what a small woman she was.

"Now, one…two…three…*hop.*"

In unison, she hopped and he lifted and she was perched onto the saddle, staring down at him. Again, knowledge shone in her eyes.

Juliet clicked her tongue, and her mount jolted into a walk.

As he watched Valentina ride away with Delilah and Juliet, he thought she must be wondering what she'd gotten herself into.

He might be wondering the same.

The initial goal remained unchanged. He would secure justice and recompense for her and her family. He was determined.

But, first, he needed to stop touching her.

Then he needed to stop sharing heated looks with her.

And he absolutely needed to stop kissing her.

He mounted his horse and glanced down at Oliver Quincy who looked lost for words for the first time in his life. Archie gave the man a silent farewell tip of the hat and set out for a cooling ride.

He may have been soaked and drenched in river muck, but he wasn't cold in the least.

In fact, he was hot.

Too hot.

Summoning his sense of self-preservation, he rode in the opposite direction of its source.

Chapter Nine

Night

ARCHIE SHOULDN'T BE in this room.

He understood that.

It was the hour of night when all was silent and the air had gone crisp and he should be in his own bedroom.

Sitting before the piano in it.

Except, tonight, when he'd sat to the instrument, the notes had refused to flow. Hands poised above the keyboard, he'd waited and waited for new notes to come. He'd thought there yet remained plenty of momentum from last night to carry him through to the end of the composition.

But one element was missing.

Valentina.

At first, he'd resisted the notion as he banged through the piece several times in the wild hope that the note beyond the last one scribbled onto the music sheet would make itself known.

But it refused.

It wanted Valentina.

So, here he was.

In her bedroom.

In the small hours of morning.

Sprawled in an armchair in the corner.

Waging a war with himself.

Would it be inconceivably rude to wake her?

Yes.

Was he already being inconceivably rude just by being here?

Also, *yes.*

Was that wrongness enough to make him leave?

No.

She'd become his muse. He needed her.

For his music.

That was what his mind kept repeating.

But his body had a different idea.

It needed her.

End of.

So, here he sat in the corner, hoping against ridiculous hope that she would wake herself.

He cleared his throat.

She didn't stir.

He shifted noisily in the chair.

She remained obstinately asleep.

He shot to his feet, and before he had a clear idea of what he was doing, he was standing beside the bed.

A hiss sounded from the foot of the bed. A tiny gray ball of fur had shot to her four paws, ready to pounce. He'd come prepared for the kitten who Juliet had dubbed Miss Hiss—a name that would likely stick. He tossed her a link of raw sausage. That should keep the bloodthirsty little creature busy for a while.

He returned his attention to Valentina. The feel of her parted mouth against his...of her waist in his hands...echoed through him. He had to clench his hands at his sides to keep from touching her.

Though only seconds had passed, the longer he stood here, the more wrong it felt. He must wake her.

"Valentina," he whispered, opting for the non-tactile approach.

Her dark fringe of eyelashes fluttered open, and she blinked. "Are you real?"

"Very much."

"I was dreaming of you," she said on a lazy, indulgent stretch.

He liked the sound of that. "And what was I doing in your dream?" He very much wanted to know.

Her eyes widened, and she came fully awake, pulling the covers up to her chin. "What is it that you want, Lord Archer?"

You, he didn't say.

"Follow me," he said instead.

"Is that an order?"

"It's actually a request." He couldn't exactly force her to be his muse.

Her gaze, luminous and searching, held his for a silent stretch of time. She saw into him down to his weakness—his *need*. It would repulse and send her fleeing into the night, surely.

She nodded, and all muscles in his body that had tensed, released. In the place of that tension soared relief. She'd agreed.

"If you'll fetch my night-rail from the bench at the dressing table..."

He only now noticed that she still held the covers to her chin, concerned for her modesty.

And why shouldn't she be?

All it would take was the single curl of her pinky, and he'd willingly ravish her.

She likely saw that in his eyes, too.

After retrieving the requested garment, he asked, "May I help you?" He hadn't intended the offer to sound lecherous, but his voice had gone into a lower register, and he thought he might.

She shook her head—wise woman—and somehow managed to clothe herself beneath the covers. He knew this, because though he'd stepped discreetly away, he watched from the periphery of his eye. He couldn't help himself. There was something about this woman that he wanted to understand, though he wasn't sure what it was.

She slid off the bed and faced him. "After you, my lord."

He pivoted and began walking, trusting—*hoping*—she would follow. Light footsteps sounded at his back as he led her through the house cast in shadow. Having her near—having her to himself—settled the tetchy feeling inside him, even as it provoked another feeling to life. A feeling rooted deep in his body—a feeling he had no business exploring.

No one had ever made him feel so.

Until her.

They entered his bedroom, its interior of white marble floor and light grays illuminated by flickering candle and moon light. It would've been more proper to use the piano in his study, but his papers and notes were all here. Besides, he and Valentina, they existed as different selves in the night.

A muted laugh sounded behind him. He tossed a glance over his shoulder. "Have I amused you?"

Night-rail dragging on the floor behind her—he supposed Tucker hadn't hemmed nightclothes—she shook her head, bemused. "Of course you have a piano in your bedroom."

It wasn't the words themselves that sparked a warm feeling inside him. It was the feeling behind them. Valentina understood his passion for music in a way not a single other person in the world did.

With her, he was known.

He wasn't certain how he felt about that, but he thought he might like it.

He leaned against the piano and watched her take the measure of his bedroom. How lovely…how soft…how appealing she was. She was a strong woman who knew her mind, but she held an openness within her, too. She understood the two weren't mutually exclusive.

She noticed the wall of bookcases that ran perpendicular to the window. "You have a library in your bedroom, too?"

He shifted on his feet. "Of sorts."

Her eyebrows crinkled in curiosity as she crossed the distance and slid a folio from a shelf. Thumbing the cover open, her eyes widened. "Oh."

He knew what she was beholding. His work. A past composition. Almost every cell in his body wanted her to close the folio and slide it back into place and forget all about it.

But a few remaining cells wanted her to keep going.

To hear the music in her head.

To appreciate it.

To love it.

No other set of eyes had ever been laid upon it.

When her gaze lifted, he saw a new expression within. She'd judged this work worthy. He attempted—and failed—to tamp down the wave of gratification that crested inside him.

"How many other pieces have you composed?"

He didn't have to think. "Thirty-two."

Her brow lifted. *"Thirty-two?"*

"Well, several of those are from childhood, so they might not count as anything anyone would want to hear."

Her head canted. "I believe they would."

Oh, how those four words entered his bloodstream and lit him up.

She held out the composition. "Will you play it for me?"

He should say *no*.

But he couldn't resist. It occurred to him he might not be able to resist any request this woman made of him.

He removed the sheets from the book and placed them on the music shelf, though he knew every note by memory. He wasn't sure if it was a blessing or a curse.

He depressed piano keys, and the notes began to coalesce into music. He'd composed this piece the summer before he'd started at Cambridge, and all the emotions of that time began to sail through him. Of the particular happiness of youth on the cusp of adulthood. Of fresh beginnings. Of anticipation.

The same feelings he experienced tonight with Valentina alone in this room with him.

She moved closer, as he'd known she would when he began playing. He felt her at his back, following the music. Though they'd never discussed it, he understood she felt music in the way he did.

To the very core of her soul.

A note sounded through the air. Not from the piano, but from behind him. From Valentina. One note flowed into another, then another, overlaying the composition with a harmony, using that glorious voice of hers. He wanted to stop playing, so he could listen as she took the composition places he hadn't dreamed of venturing, but he couldn't. In this moment in time, her music and his music were one.

Tonight, he was her muse.

Together, they were creating something worthwhile—something special.

When he neared the end of one sheet, she leaned around him to turn the page. Separated by mere inches, he caught her scent. *Lemon and roses and night and woman.*

Then she flipped to the last page, and he was playing the final notes. The music drifted into the night, leaving a deafening silence in its wake. He shifted around so he straddled the piano bench, facing her. She stared down at him only a few feet away, her cheeks flushed and her eyes bright with the particular joy of creation.

"Why don't you play in public?" she asked.

Archie felt his most charming smile—the one reserved for the world outside this room—rear its ugly head. He could hate himself for it. To use artifice with Valentina felt wrong. But she was veering too close to truths that felt safer kept hidden away. He laughed, almost a scoff, dismissive.

Her eyebrows drew together. She wasn't charmed. "You have a gift."

"*I*, Miss Hart," he said, "have a title."

She needed to understand that.

"And you think that's all you should be?"

He shrugged a shoulder. "It's all the world thinks I am."

"Because that's all you've presented it."

"Because that's all they want. They want their sunshine in a smile."

The question in her eyes released, and in its place entered certainty. He wasn't sure he liked that.

"Ah," she said.

He most definitely didn't like it. "*Ah?*"

"They like the Lord Archer—"

"Archie," he corrected.

"They like the Archie who is always up for a lark and a laugh."

"Who wouldn't?"

The question was flimsy, at best. He felt its protection giving way.

"And you like being liked."

"I'm not unique in that."

"You think the world only wants to see the light."

"Do you want to see that dark?"

"I'm seeing him now."

"Do you like him?"

"I believe I do."

To be seen. To be known. To be liked for the parts of himself he kept carefully hidden from view…

"You are overtired, methinks," he said, needing a safe distance from the intimacy fast forming between them. "Perhaps this was a mistake."

He was dismissing her. They both knew it. But her feet remained planted. She wasn't finished. "You are an artist."

"I am a viscount, who shall be an earl someday."

"You cannot simply shut away and deny the largest part of yourself. You cannot be happy unless you're authentic to who you are in your heart."

He laughed, again. How he was coming to hate the sound of his charming laugh. "I am almost too authentic for my own good. Ask anyone."

Valentina remained unmoved. She wasn't letting him charm his way out of this conversation. "But *this* is you." She indicated the piano, the thirty-one composition folios lining his bookcase, the one on the music stand. *"He* matters. He may matter most."

Her ideas took instant root inside him, and her words were their nourishment. Of a sudden, he wanted—*needed*—more of them.

He wanted—*needed...craved*—this intimacy that existed between them.

He felt he must warn her.

He must give her one last chance to flee.

"You don't understand the effect of your words on me."

"Don't I?" she asked, low and certain and...inviting.

A feeling that he'd kept carefully banked breached his defenses.

Still, he must resist. "You don't."

She reached out and picked up his hand where it rested on the keyboard and placed it at the curve of her waist. Where it had rested earlier today. "I understand more than you think, my lord."

"Valentina," he rasped. "I'm only a man."

"And *I* am only a woman."

He shook his head. *"You* are temptation personified."

"And don't you want to pluck me?"

Had she truly spoken those words with *that* meaning running below them?

The intention in her eyes said *yes*.

Though he shouldn't...

Though he would surely regret it on the morrow...

He would pluck her since she'd asked.

Chapter Ten

THE WORDS SPILLING from Valentina's mouth... She didn't understand why she needed so badly to speak them.

They would lead her down the path to ruin, if she wasn't careful. Except...

She was too far gone down that particular path to be careful.

From the moment she'd opened her eyes to find Archie beside her bed, metamorphosed from her dream, she'd understood the inevitability of this moment.

The hand at her waist instinctively tightened. Strong and capable, those fingers of his. And when he tugged, she swayed forward, placing her hand on top of his, the feel of his bare skin beneath hers enough to send a flame of heat through her. She guided him up, so together, they pulled back a panel of her nightrail.

She shrugged one shoulder then the other, and the garment loosed and fell to a silken puddle on the floor, leaving her clad in naught but a flimsy chemise.

His pupils flared, pushing his irises into thin blue rings. *Desire.* Her body pulsed with it.

He cupped the back of her head, pulling her down so her lips were separated from his by the scantest sliver of air. "It's not too late to turn back," he spoke into that slender space, his lips brushing against hers, tempting her.

"Oh, but it is," she said, pushing forward, at last, claiming his mouth with hers. Her head went light and her knees weak. His hands slid down the length of her body. She groaned when he slipped his tongue inside her mouth, leading her more fully into the carnality of the moment.

The Lord Archer she knew in the daylight was all lightness and air.

But this Lord Archer... His presence possessed a solid physicality capable of plumbing depths.

And, oh, how she wanted her depths plumbed.

The dark intention within his eyes promised he could.

His mouth found her neck, and a moan escaped her as his fingers trailed beneath her chemise, and before she knew what he was about, he'd pulled back and had it over her head, flung away.

He went utterly still as he took in her naked form. "Valentina," fell from his mouth, "what a body you have."

To see her effect on him, it touched a place of deep feminine power.

"May I touch you?" he asked.

"You've been touching me." And a little more.

"That was before."

She threaded her fingers through his and lifted, bringing his hand to her breast. He squeezed, and she gasped. "Do that again."

A wicked smile curled the corner of his mouth as he took her nipple between forefinger and thumb. "Your wish is my command."

He squeezed again, and—*oh*—that felt even better.

"Where else would you like me to touch you?" he asked.

He knew where she wanted to be touched, but she'd started this game and he wanted to play, her way.

"I...I..."

Oh, could she speak her desires aloud?

Was she so shameless?

"I want you to place your mouth on my breast."

She was.

A laugh rumbled deep in his chest. As he squeezed one nipple with his fingers, he took the other with his mouth. "Oooh," poured from her in a long, sensuous groan. Sensation, wild and glorious, soared through her as he suckled, nipped, swirled his tongue and flicked it against her.

And she'd thought his hands were talented.

She squeezed her thighs together, for the sensation that fizzed through her had settled there—in the secret place only she knew.

His head tipped back. "Is there anywhere else you would like me to touch you?"

She nearly whimpered. His words touched *that* place.

Could she do it? Could she guide his hand there?

How badly did she want it?

How badly did she *need* it?

She took the hand clutched at her waist and led it, down...across the flat of her stomach...down the dark curls of her mons pubis, his long, masculine fingers inciting a blaze of heat along her skin.

Though she ached—*throbbed*—for more of his touch—*there*—she stopped, of a sudden uncertain.

He seemed to understand. His gaze met hers. "Place your knee on my thigh," he said, his voice a gravelly rasp.

She did as he instructed, and his thumb slid along the slit of her sex. "So wet," he murmured against her belly, trailing kisses there.

Her eyes shut, and her head arced back. The only place she existed in the world were the places he touched—the indent of her waist...the flat of her belly...a hard, sensitive nipple...*her quim*. His thumb pressed against a nub that came alive with instant sensation. She gasped, and her knee involuntarily opened wider. She needed more of his touch—*there*. Another of his clever fingers moved along her slit and then—*oh*—entered her, even as his thumb continued touching *her*.

"Oh," she gasped, as he began stroking in and out of her, his long finger thick and so talented. The very essence of her being was condensed into this one place, even as she felt suspended above it.

Of their own will, her hips began to move, creating a rhythm with him. A feeling tensed inside her and held her in its grip. A tension unlike any she'd ever experienced, that insisted she abandon herself to the pleasure he offered.

This feeling was a promise. The promise of an end, her body understood that. If only she could find the way.

But this man, the one who had taken her body in hand, he knew how to get her there.

The tension tightened its grasp, and the breath caught in her throat as she felt suspended between two worlds—that of the physical and another place that taunted and teased just out of reach, as she balanced on the edge of the unknown until...

It broke inside her, all that had been tensed releasing on an unruly wave that washed through her. "Archie," she cried, arcing into him, demanding more as abandon tipped her beyond the boundaries of the physical.

She wasn't sure how long she remained poised like that, but eventually the race of her heart slowed, and she opened her eyes to find his head angled back, his gaze fast upon her.

"How did you do that?" she asked—*demanded*.

He laughed.

"You're as clever as you think you are." She was serious.

"Valentina," he said. "Do you trust me?"

The answer was instinctive. "Yes."

His finger slid from her, and she moaned at the loss of him.

He stood and in a single efficient motion swept her into his arms. Her face nestled against the crook of his neck as he carried her across the room, lay her on the bed, and stood back. It only struck her now that she was entirely naked while he was fully clothed in trousers and shirt.

She propped herself up onto her elbows. Her breasts stood high and proud on her chest. The hunger in his eyes deepened.

He rather liked her voluptuous breasts.

Well, they liked him back.

He slid the shirt over his head, and her gaze swept slowly across him. Tall and angular was this man, but muscled, too, and not an ounce of excess on him. The defined muscles of his chest were covered in a fuzz of blond hair that led down the ridged muscles of his stomach, and even further below where his fingers were loosening the fall of his trousers. Clearly delineated beneath superfine wool was the rigid outline of his manhood. Then fabric dropped, and it sprang free.

A shiver streaked through her.

Long, thick, turgid… Her body wanted *that*.

Inside her.

He dispatched the trousers with a few movements. He was gorgeous, this man. So golden and light, and yet it was the dark promise in his eyes that sent a shard of desire straight through her.

Gone was the Lord Archer out to charm the world with his smile. In its place was a wicked curl of the mouth, and a steady intent in his eyes. To be the desire of such a man was nearly as seductive as his touch. *Nearly.*

She came to her knees as he stepped to the edge of the bed. He reached for her—one hand drawing her in for a kiss, the other clutching her hip, pulling her so her body met the length of his, his hard manhood pressed against her belly. Twin threads of desire and anticipation trembled through her at the feel of his smooth skin beneath her hands, the hot tangle of his tongue with hers.

Hands tightened around her, and he lay her down beneath him. One elbow planted to the side of her head, he hovered above her, his fingers tracing across her breasts and down her stomach to the mound of her sex.

"Valentina," he whispered against her mouth.

It was only then she realized her eyes were closed. She'd become a being composed entirely of sensation. She found him staring down at her.

"You can touch me."

And it struck her.

What he was giving her, she could give him.

Now wasn't the time to be bashful.

In this bed, together, they were equals.

They were man and woman.

Madly in lust with one another.

And she knew exactly which part of him she would like to touch first. She reached up and ran her fingers through tousled golden curls. "As soft as I thought they'd be."

"You've been thinking about my curls?"

"All the ladies must."

She smoothed her hands across his wide shoulders, muscles tensed as they held him above her. They weren't the thick muscles of some men, but lean and sinewy as they tapered into strong arms. Then her fingertips were trailing down his fuzzed chest...down his stomach composed entirely of ridged muscles. The feel of his skin, smooth and warm. The feel of the muscle beneath, steel and unyielding. For all this man was glib charm, in this moment he was all solid man.

Her hands ventured farther. To his taut arse. She gave it a squeeze. Humor flickered in his eyes.

"You can touch me," he rasped, serious, imploring.

She knew the *me* of which he spoke. His manhood, hard and thick and waiting...for her.

The heat that pulsed through her wasn't from a blush, but from a desire to do exactly as he implored.

Touch him, as he'd touched her.

Fingertips that trembled traced down his hard, velvet length, and she nearly gasped at the craving that sparked within her. A groan sounded at the back of his throat, only emboldening her. Her hand wrapped around him, and the breath caught in his chest. To have this man so completely in her thrall... Seductive, feminine power slid through her.

His fingers reached down and grazed along her slit. She, too, was in his power. This abandon to each other was unexpected, and she wanted more of it. To give over completely to whatever it was that bound them.

But, oh, how hard and full he was in her hand.

How wet she was for him. "I need you inside me," she uttered. Now it was her turn to implore.

On primal instinct, her legs widened, and he moved between. His gaze met and held hers, the tip of his manhood pressed against her sex. Her hips angled up, straining for what he withheld. On a slow, deliberate stroke, he began entering her, stretching her as he filled her.

He suddenly stopped, alarm in his eyes. "You're a virgin."

"And?"

"And I've never been with a virgin."

"Then it'll be your first time, too."

He stared down at her, doubts unshaken.

So, she took his face in her hands and drew him down so his lips touched hers, the act intimate—almost as intimate as the other act they were poised upon. "I need to be filled by you," she whispered against his mouth.

"Valentina," he rasped, his arse tightening as he pushed through her maidenhead.

She gasped at the spike of pain.

"Are you hurt?" he asked, concern clouding the clear blue of his eyes.

She shook her head. "I feel like..." Oh, how to say what she felt... "It feels like everything all at once."

And yet she wanted more.

His hips began to move, one slow, testing stroke after another, allowing her to adjust to the feel of him. She'd never felt so...*full*. A bead of sweat dripped down his chin onto her chest as she sought more of this pleasure mixed with pain, and he delivered.

A feeling—the feeling from minutes ago—again began to

climb inside her. It tensed and coiled and left her no option but to center her entire being toward the satisfaction of it. This feeling, it placed demands on her, and oh, how she wanted to satisfy it.

Her arms tightened around him, and she groaned her frustration—her *need*—into his neck.

He angled his head so he met her eye. "Valentina, you can trust me. I'll get you there."

His mouth began trailing along the column of her neck, tightening her nipples, making her wild beneath him. And still he thrust into her, an unrelenting drive that filled her and sent waves of lust licking through her, even as more was promised...

Feeling burst inside her, lightning streaking through her sex as it pulsed around his hard manhood. His gaze went interior as his own climb toward release overtook him, and he withdrew from her, rolling to the side and spilling his seed outside her.

He collapsed back, joining her in this state that felt as if her body was floating in a cloud of ether. How could such a deeply physical act be so completely beyond the bounds of the corporeal at the same time?

And yet with each breath and slowing beat of her heart, she sank back into her body and the reality of the man beside her.

She turned her head and found his gaze already upon her. "You're no longer a virgin."

She could see it was weighing on him. "It's different for us."

His eyebrows crinkled together. "*Us* who?"

"The riff-raff."

His jaw clenched. He didn't like that answer.

"A woman's maidenhead isn't as important to my class."

It was mostly true. If there was a babe, well, that was a different matter. But, thankfully, he'd taken precautions.

Her words, however, did seem to assuage him a small bit as he gathered her close and snugged her into the curl of his body. "We'll discuss it tomorrow," he muttered into her hair. Not long after, his breathing became even in the cadence of sleep.

But Valentina's gaze remained obstinately fixed on the canopy above.

We'll discuss it tomorrow.

And with which Lord Archer would she be discussing *it*?

The one always on the lookout for a lark and a laugh?

Or the one whose arm was presently providing a pillow for her head? The one with hidden depths?

Or was it possible they were one and the same?

Chapter Eleven

Next day

ARCHIE KNEW BEFORE he opened his eyes.

She was gone.

Morning sun peeking through parted bed curtains, he slitted his eyes open. The space beside him—where Valentina should have been—lay empty, no longer even warm. She'd been gone a while, that cold space told him.

Last night…

She'd been a virgin.

This morning…

She wasn't.

Right.

It's different for us.

That simply wasn't true.

Everyone had feelings and desires, wants and needs. Class made no difference.

No, Miss Valentina Hart had been deflecting. She hadn't wanted to have a difficult conversation. And though he wasn't exactly known for wading into waters fraught with difficulty—clear, smooth-running streams were much his preference—he wasn't letting her not have this difficult conversation. Surely, they could come to some sort of arrangement.

The instant the word *arrangement* formed in his mind, he felt immediate revulsion. That word put him on a level with certain lords he didn't particularly like, or respect.

He swept the coverlet away and pushed out of bed. Twenty minutes later, he was entering the morning room, fully, impeccably dressed, a smile to greet the day on his mouth. But the room was empty of Valentina, and everyone else for that matter. He didn't have a pocket watch to consult, but it only now occurred to him that it might be early morning. The light was still golden, and the air yet held that specific stillness.

A servant carrying a tray of croissants entered. The surprised lift of her eyebrows when she spotted him was all the confirmation Archie needed. He was definitely early to breakfast.

Further, he wasn't only early.

He was eager, anticipation racing through his veins at the prospect of greeting the new day with Valentina.

He took his customary seat at the table and allowed himself to be served his usual morning meal—pot of piping hot coffee, toast, eggs, tomatoes, and black pudding. He was absolutely ravenous this morning.

A small silver tray bearing a note appeared to his right. He sliced the missive open with a butter knife and scanned its contents. He set the note down, a feeling of satisfaction sweeping through him. Everything was falling into place concerning the swindle of Lord Nestor. Tomorrow, Valentina's family's money would be secured. And then...

Well, he would never see her again.

He pushed his plate away, his appetite suddenly vanished.

The sound of chatty voices grew near. He'd just slid the note into the interior pocket of his morning coat when Delilah and Juliet entered the room. Their eyebrows lifted to the coffered ceiling when they noticed him.

"Brother," said Delilah, sliding into her chair, "you're up and about awfully early."

"Or are you still awake from last night?" asked Juliet, all wide-eyed innocence and anything but.

"Very amusing," he said, dry. His gaze flicked toward the

doorway. *Empty.*

Perhaps Valentina was in need of a lie-in.

After last night.

The longer he was awake the more he felt like a rogue. What had he been thinking?

Five…ten…fifteen minutes later, he, Delilah, and Juliet were in the middle of breakfast and a story Delilah had heard about the Marchioness of Wyndham's wig becoming entangled with a tenacious gooseberry bush during an assignation with a soldier in Regent's Park.

"No doubt a diverting story, Delilah," began Archie.

"It is," said Delilah. "You should wait for the ending. It doesn't turn out how you'd expect."

Archie cleared his throat as nonchalantly as possible. "Any news of Miss Hart this morning?"

Two sets of eyebrows lifted in his direction. He hated when Delilah and Juliet did that. Never mind cousins, these two were practically twins.

"Yes," said Delilah, and left it at that as she speared a sausage.

Juliet, bless her, took pity on him. "She's gone."

It was just as well Archie had only picked at his meal, for it all felt ready to come back up. He'd scared Valentina off. That was the long and short of it. He'd never been any good at keeping his desires in check.

And he'd desired Miss Valentina Hart from the instant he'd laid eyes on her. He'd needed to possess her.

And he had.

And now…

He needed to find her.

And his sister and cousin knew something more than they were saying. He saw it in their eyes. "Now, Juliet," he began, thinking she might take pity on him again. "Perhaps you could tell me where."

Juliet shook her head slowly. "Miss Hart spoke with Delilah."

"Remember, she said to call her Valentina," inserted Delilah.

Her head canted with mischief. "But perhaps not you, Arch."

Though he was desperate to find Valentina, he mustn't appear too eager, particularly when that feline smile was curling about Delilah's mouth.

"Shall we play our usual game?" she asked. "Or shall I get on with it and tell you now?"

"Now, if you wouldn't mind too much."

She shrugged one shoulder. "She's gone to visit her family. It's Sunday."

"What's the significance of Sunday?"

"Keep up, Archie." Delilah rolled her eyes. "Valentina is visiting her family to assure them she's alive and well. Juliet and I are caring for Miss Hiss today."

As if she'd only been awaiting her cue, the kitten sauntered into the room with a haughty swish of her tail, hopped onto an empty chair, and began licking her fluffy gray fur with queenly dignity.

Archie returned his attention to Delilah. "In Hampstead, correct?"

"Indeed," supplied Juliet.

"I thought Valentina told Delilah," said Archie. Truly, these two could exasperate the feathers off a chicken.

"Well, I was standing right there."

Archie didn't have time for Delilah and Juliet's games. He shot to his feet. "I've, erm, just remembered an appointment."

Delilah pulled out her pocket watch. She was the only Windermere possessed of any association with time. Something to do with her chosen vocation of acting. "At eight in the morning?"

Was it that early? Still... "Yes."

As one, Delilah and Juliet's eyes narrowed on him. He wasn't sure which would ask the question that had formed in both their minds. All he could do was brace himself. It was Juliet who spoke. "If you don't mind me asking, what are your intentions toward dearest Valentina?"

Sudden heat flushed through Archie. "As a matter of fact, I do mind you asking."

Two sets of eyebrows lifted.

Archie wasn't known for being touchy. Quite the opposite, in fact. He should've given Delilah and Juliet a rakish smile and let them think what they liked. But he couldn't.

Not when it concerned Valentina.

He walked from the room with a measured stride. But the instant he was out of sight, his feet picked up their pace until he'd struck into a flat-out run. He had a Valentina to find somewhere between here and Hampstead.

And not a second to lose.

*

VALENTINA LET HER legs dangle off the back of the donkey cart and inhaled early morning sunshine, all golden and fresh.

It felt good to get out of London for the day. To return to her real life. The life she'd been living at Casa Windermere certainly wasn't real life. Or, at least, not *her* real life.

She needed to see her family, to bring them reassurance that she was well. They hadn't been thrilled with her idea to seek out Lord Nestor, but they hadn't been able to stop her. She'd simply had to do something—*anything*—to help fix the situation.

Recently spoken words returned to her.

"You're wilder than you think, you know."

She hadn't known.

But now she certainly did.

Last night, she'd been absolutely wild for the man who had spoken those words.

And this morning?

She might still be.

Which was another reason it had been imperative to get out of his house for the day.

A cart wheel hit a deep rut in the road, and a loud, "Argh!" lurched from her lungs as she grabbed onto the sides to keep from being dumped onto the road. The farmer who had offered the ride likely wouldn't have noticed, for he was quite deaf.

A coach-and-four appeared around the bend they'd rounded a few minutes ago, charging up the road like the demons of hell were nipping at its wheels. She wasn't sure how the coachman expected to move around the farmer, who couldn't hear its approach, which she kept an increasingly alarmed eye upon. The carriage wasn't slowing, but rather increasing its speed. Only when the lead pair of horses had come within a few yards of the donkey cart did the coachman rein in the team.

Valentina gripped the cart tighter. What was this about?

Then from the side of the carriage poked a head—a head of golden, tousled curls…

Archie.

Valentina couldn't help herself. She laughed. It was just such a very Archie thing to do.

"Valentina," he shouted. "Do you need a ride?"

"I have one," she shouted back. It was merely a statement of the obvious.

His jaw took on a mulish set. He'd become determined, and a determined Archie was an implacable Archie, and an implacable Archie was a relentless Archie.

She knew from recent experience.

Her body heated up by a few degrees.

Still, the farmer hadn't any notion of the coach-and-four at his rear. Valentina supposed she should alert him, for Archie wasn't going anywhere. She tapped the farmer's shoulder. He glanced around to discover the unexpected situation at his back before guiding the donkey cart to the side of the road, clearly expecting the lord's coach-and-four to pass.

But it didn't. Instead, it stopped, too, and out stepped an impeccably dressed lord in a forest-green morning coat, buff superfine trousers, and snow-white cravat. The Platonic ideal of an English lord stood before them.

The farmer held his hat in his hands and shuffled his feet.

"Now, I don't know what this be about, milord," he said, wary. "But I'll not be wantin' trouble."

Archie nodded respectfully and held out his hand to Valentina. Her hands remained clutched around the reticule in her lap. "Why are you here?" she asked.

"I wanted to make sure—"

"Now, off with ye," shouted the farmer. Valentina realized he was shouting at her. "I don't have truck with lords and their fancy women."

Valentina supposed she was the fancy woman in this scenario. Her only option was to vacate her perch on the cart. The farmer flapped the reins and set his donkey into motion.

Now, she was stuck in the middle of the road. Annoyance flared at the man standing before her with a lopsided grin on his mouth. "Now you've lost me my ride."

He jutted his chin toward his coach-and-four. "I've a better one."

Like that, last night lifted its thoroughly pleasured head. Was a double meaning located in his words? She searched his eyes and found not a hint of salaciousness. Of course, that meant nothing with this man.

"Shall we?" he asked.

She exhaled a deep, resigned sigh, and he took her hand to help her into his carriage. It was the most luxurious carriage she'd ever encountered. *Of course.* It was even scented of cloves and spice. Of *him.*

She sat on the plush bench opposite him. After last night, she'd wondered how she would face him again. But it was shockingly easy.

Was it so shocking, though?

She'd wanted to do what she'd done with him—desperately. It wasn't only about his charm and handsome exterior. It was those depths of his that few likely saw.

"Why are you here?" she asked conversationally.

"Word has it you're paying a visit to your family, and I

thought it would be a lark to join you."

She believed him. Yet more lurked below, as always did with this man. She decided to let it pass. "My family aren't like yours." He needed to understand the sort of family she came from. "They're not larkers."

His charming smile didn't yield. "I'm certain we'll rub along like bees and flowers." He cleared his throat. "Perhaps not the most apt metaphor."

Or was it too apt?

She shook off the question. She doubted not that he would be unequal to the challenge of charming her family. Well, perhaps not Mama. Mama was decidedly *un*-charmable. It was one of her most endearing characteristics.

"My question remains, Lord Archer," said Valentina. "Why are you here?"

"Archie," he corrected. He glanced out the window. "You'll be at the musicale tonight?"

Ah. Now she understood. He thought she'd left, for good. She saw his question for what it was. A crack. An insecurity revealed. "I shall," she said.

"Because the outswindle depends on it," he said. He'd returned his gaze to her. It burned with intensity.

"I'll be there, Archie."

This seemed to settle something inside him, and he nodded. "You don't need time to ready yourself with all the perfumes, ointments, and tinctures ladies use to ready themselves?"

She shrugged. "Half an hour will do."

He laughed. She detected relief in that laugh. "You truly aren't from my world."

"Is that a bad thing?" Why had she asked such a question? She shouldn't. And yet... Something in her needed to know.

All traces of his charming smile fell away. "Not at all. Very much the opposite."

Last night was suddenly between them, its substance so dense it was nearly a solid object.

In the new light of morning, she didn't feel as she'd thought she would. It was this absence of shame. Though she may come to regret her relations with this man someday, it wouldn't be because she regretted what they'd done last night.

"Are you feeling..." He looked utterly nonplussed. "Erm, *rested?*"

Valentina opted for the honest answer. "Not particularly."

He laughed, and the tension released from the carriage.

Outside the window, she could see they were now rolling down the high street of Hampstead, familiar shops to either side passing by. "You can instruct the coachman to let us out there." She pointed toward the shopfront with the word *APOTHECARY* emblazoned in brass above its front door. "Our family's quarters are behind and above the shop."

Valentina felt a smile form about her mouth as she landed on cobblestones whose every curve and divot she knew by heart. "Home," she said. "Follow me."

She pushed the front door open, and the bell above announced her arrival with a little jingle. The shop was far from its typically quiet self. Instead, she and Archie found a hive of activity. Then she remembered what today was. Twice a year Papa set aside a Sunday to make repairs to the shop and give it a general spiff up.

"Valentina," called out one of her brothers—Antonio—with a wave. Three others lifted their heads in greeting, but didn't pause in their duties.

Papa's head appeared above his prize walnut counter, and a smile broadened across his face. "Valentina!" His eyes shifted, and his smile dipped a fraction, his warm gaze narrowing with assessment. "And who do you have with you?"

She'd known this was coming. Of course, Papa would wonder about this man she'd brought home.

She was clearing her throat to make introductions when Archie stepped forward, face lit by his charming smile, which he'd wisely turned down a few degrees, hand extended over the counter for a shake. "Archie Windermere," he said. "Pleased to make your acquaintance, Mr. Hart."

Papa's eyebrows lifted. It wasn't only Valentina who'd noticed he'd left the *Lord* off his name. He was just so utterly and completely a lord, no disguising it. Still, Papa took Archie's proffered hand and gave it a shake, even as he flicked a quick glance toward Valentina. She could try to explain Archie to Papa, but best to let Archie explain himself.

"Now," he said, rubbing his hands together. "Where can I pitch in?" He'd already shed his morning coat and was rolling up his sleeves.

A measure of appreciation entered Papa's eyes. He wasn't about to turn down an offer of free labor. "Luca," he called out to Valentina's youngest brother. "Show Mr. Windermere—"

"Archie."

Papa's eyebrows crinkled quizzically. "Show *Archie* the drawer you're repairing." He pointed toward the floor-to-ceiling wall of drawers of various sizes housing all manner of powders, herbs, serums, syrups, and tinctures.

Archie flashed Valentina a grin as he passed, leaving her with Papa. But before Papa could question her about the friendly stranger, a voice claimed her attention. "Valentina, *mia cara.*"

Mama stood in the doorway that led to the kitchen at the back of the shop, a question in her serious brown eyes.

"Mama," said Valentina, crossing the distance between them, submitting to a lengthy hug and a kiss on each cheek.

After Mama had properly assessed Valentina for wellness, and found her in good health, she glanced pointedly in Archie's direction, then said, "Come with me."

Valentina followed Mama through the scrumptious-smelling kitchen warm with baking bread to the small back garden, where she'd been pruning her herb garden. Mama handed Valentina a basket for collecting clippings, lowered to her knees, and returned to her task. Scents of basil, rosemary, thyme, and sage swirled through the mid-morning air. Valentina's stomach rumbled in anticipation of the meal Mama would prepare with these herbs.

"Who is that man?" asked Mama. She wasn't one to mince words.

But...how to explain Archie?

Simply and honestly. Mama would see through anything else.

"He's the man who will see our family's savings returned."

Mama's direct gaze cut sideways to meet Valentina's. "You truly believe this?"

Valentina's answer was instantaneous. "Yes."

Mama's eyebrows lifted. She only ever believed a promise after it had become tangible substance that she could hold in her hands.

"Without any doubt," continued Valentina. She believed Archie capable of anything he set his mind to.

"He's a lord?" Mama almost spat the question.

"Yes." Valentina had known this could be a stumbling block.

Mama's gaze fixed on a point over Valentina's shoulder. She turned and saw Archie and Papa standing in the kitchen, talking. Nay, not merely talking. The two were having what appeared to be a conversation of some intensity. Then Archie held out a white square of paper. A calling card.

Valentina felt her eyebrows draw together. What was Archie about?

"You're certain about this man?" asked Mama. "You trust him?"

Valentina nodded, distracted.

Mama took her hand. "And I trust you, Valentina. I trust your heart." She came to her feet and dusted off her skirts. "Now, let us cook."

Chapter Twelve

ARCHIE WASN'T SURE he'd eaten so much food in a single sitting in all his life—one steady course after another—antipasti, followed by primi pasti, followed by secondi, followed by formaggi, followed by dolci—with Mrs. Hart saying when she'd noticed his gustatory gusto flagging, *"L'appetito vien mangiando."*

The appetite comes while you are eating.

He only just didn't rub his stomach as he sat across from Valentina, the carriage rattling down country lanes just outside London. A man must maintain his mystique.

For her part, she'd been gazing out the window these last ten minutes, watching the countryside roll by, *thinking*. He didn't mind her thinking, but only if she shared those thoughts with him.

Her eyes shifted and met his. She'd caught him squarely in the act of staring. He didn't mind. She must have an inkling of her effect on him by now, what with his ravishment of her last night.

"My family likes you," she said.

"I rather like them, too," he said. And it was the truth. A big, boisterous family, Valentina's father and brothers had readily welcomed him into their midst as he'd helped with whatever task they found for him. Her mother was a tougher prospect. But he might have won her over by clearing every plate she set in front of him.

"You only say that because of Mama's food."

"Her tiramisu is nothing short of a revelation."

"I have a question for you." Valentina was watching him very closely, a trait he now knew she got from her mother. "What were you speaking about with Papa?"

"Tomorrow."

"Tomorrow?"

"At Epsom."

"The racecourse where you've arranged to meet Lord Nestor?"

Archie nodded. "I wanted to give your father and anyone else who'd been swindled by Nestor the chance to be there when justice is meted out."

Her demeanor softened. "That's very thoughtful of you."

Archie shrugged, dismissive.

"Not many people know that about you, do they?"

He wasn't sure he liked the direction this conversation was taking. "People generally see what they want to see in a person."

"And you play upon those assumptions to your advantage."

He definitely didn't like this direction. "And what advantage is that?"

"To remain hidden."

Oh, this woman… She saw too much.

Too much?

No.

He wanted to be seen by her.

He also wanted…

Her.

His best wicked smile curled about his mouth, and he reached down into the footwell between them and scooped up her right foot.

She gasped and tried to reclaim the appendage. He held tight.

"What are you doing?" she exclaimed.

"Your feet must ache from all the walking you did earlier."

"I caught a ride on the donkey cart two streets over from Casa Windermere."

"Oh, you poor thing," he commiserated. He began untying her boot laces.

"*Archie.*" She tried to keep the scold on her face, but ultimately gave up the struggle and laughed.

He slid the boot off her foot and began rubbing her sole. He sensed her tension melting by slow increments. How long before she was a puddle in the footwell?

He reached for her other foot, which she offered with nary a struggle. When he interrupted his ministrations to untie the laces of her other boot, she gave a small cry of protest.

"Has no one ever rubbed your feet?"

She shook her head.

His fingers got to work, and her eyes drifted shut. He liked providing her bliss. In fact... "Do you know what would make this foot rub even better?"

"Hmm," was her reply.

"If we removed your stockings."

Her eyes fluttered open. "Is that so?"

"Skin on skin makes all the difference," he said, low and velvet.

He hadn't started this as a seduction, but it was very quickly turning into one.

And Valentina didn't appear resistant to the idea.

"I'm content to defer to your expertise, my lord."

Her other boot fell to the floor.

A foot in each hand, he dug thumbs and fingers into muscle, pulling moans and groans and soulful sighs from her as he moved up ankles and calves. That hint of a wicked smile curling about her mouth... It was new. She might have learned it from him.

He felt no small amount of gratification that he was the man to pull that smile from her. A possessive feeling surged through him.

Her wicked smile belonged to him.

What a novel feeling—this need to possess…to claim.

For all his aristocratic titles and well-bred manners, was he not so very far removed from warlord ancestors who claimed and possessed as their right?

A thought for another time perhaps.

For now, here was Valentina, in his hands, looking very much like she wanted nothing more than to be claimed and possessed.

His hands moved up to her thighs, smooth and firm beneath his fingers. He slid forward and off his bench entirely, coming to his knees. From beneath her eyelashes, she watched him kneeling before her. He her supplicant; she his goddess.

Her skirts bunched to her upper thighs, a band of skin showing above her gray stockings. A stretch of skin that was temptation itself.

Archie's mouth went dry.

And he knew exactly how to wet it.

Though she looked more than willing, he needed a *yes* from her. "Can I do something else for you?" he asked.

"You can do anything to me," she said. A light blush turned her cheeks dusky rose, but her eyes burned bright with assent. Perhaps she'd shocked herself, but she wanted what he offered.

And it was the latter that was winning out.

"Be careful what you wish for," he said.

"With you?" Again, her full lips curved into that new, wicked smile of hers. "Always."

His hands inched forward, savoring the feel of her creamy thighs. He ducked beneath her skirts and heard a gasp.

"Archie!"

He chuckled.

"What are you—"

His tongue found her quim and slowly dragged along its slit. She inhaled a sharp gasp and wasn't able to finish her sentence. He breathed deeply of lemon and rose and woman and coitus. A long, languorous moan poured from her, and her knees parted wider. She'd given over completely to him.

One hand found his shoulder and gripped it tight. He imagined her other arm thrown above her head arced back in abandon as his tongue found the sensitive nub of her sex and two fingers entered her silken center. *Wet...so wet.* His cock couldn't get any harder as his fingers slid in and out of her, and his tongue flicked against her.

"I want to see you," she said.

The hand not gripping his shoulder grabbed her skirts, pulling and bunching them up. His head emerged, and up the length of her body his gaze met hers, lust-glazed and hungry for more of the pleasure he was delivering to her.

Archie found himself in the grip of an unexpected feeling. He wasn't simply a tool to be used for her pleasure. She wanted that, of course, but she sought more. She sought connection.

With him.

Of a sort different from the union of their two bodies. This connection probed deeper, to a place he only explored with his music, never with another person. But with Valentina...

It felt right.

This was intimacy.

His gaze fixed onto hers, and he concentrated the tip of his tongue upon that explosive little nub where all sensation sparked. "Oh, yes," escaped from her parted mouth, and her eyes glazed over as she drew into the interior place where climax hovered just out of reach, taunting her, teasing her, with its promise of pleasure.

And it was down to him to deliver that pleasure.

His fingers pressed deeper inside her wet warmth as his tongue concentrated against her sensitive nub. She moaned. She sighed. She cried out in little gasps of want and frustration and utter need. She angled her hips and squirmed against him, demanding more. She knew what she wanted, but he knew how to give it to her.

Of a sudden, her back arched and her eyes squeezed shut and

she tensed beneath him. One...two...three more flicks of his tongue, and she broke, her climax pulsing against him, around his fingers.

He wanted to be inside her, feel her sweet warmth tight around him. But this had been for her. Slowly, he pulled away and sat back on his haunches as he tugged her skirts so they fell primly to her ankles. But not before bussing each of her creamy thighs with a parting kiss.

He resumed his seat on the opposite bench. It could almost be believed that nothing had just occurred. Except the flush rising from her décolletage and pinking her cheeks would fool no one. The woman looked ravished and sated.

Ravished?

Not quite, his cock protested.

She canted her head in question. "Why are you all the way over there?"

"That was for you," he said.

She bit her bottom lip, and her gaze fell to his lap, where his cock was making quite a spectacle of itself beneath buff superfine. "Oh, you have more to offer me than that, Lord Archer."

She shifted forward and slinked—there was no other word for the way she moved—across the footwell separating them, all the while bunching up her skirts with one hand and placing the other onto his shoulder. One knee, then the other, moved onto the bench to either side of him, so she straddled his thighs and came to hover above him, her dark, luminous gaze holding his.

How beautiful and sensuous she was.

His, returned that voice that demanded to claim and possess.

He cupped the back of her head and brought her mouth toward his. "*Hoyden*," he muttered against her lips just before his tongue probed and claimed her.

Nimble fingers reached between them, and she had the fall of his trousers open with a few flicks. He chuckled. "Quick learner."

As feminine fingertips feathered up and down his length, sensation flew through him. Her hand, warm and firm, wrapped around him and stroked. A groan poured from the depths of his chest—of his very soul. "Turnabout is only fair play," she muttered. He felt her smile against his mouth. "But I need you inside me."

His hands clutched her hips, lifting her, his cock poised below the entrance of her sex. Bliss awaited them, but it was hers to decide and take. Sweat pinpricked his skin, as anticipation built inside him.

Inch by slow, careful inch, she lowered onto him, her quim stretching around him, taking him inside. Oh, the slick, tight feel of her. When she'd taken all she could handle for the moment, she paused, her eyes closed, her mouth parted, her breath quick and shallow.

His mouth found her neck, and his hands her bodice, pushing it low, giving her breasts leave to spill over in all their voluptuous glory. He cupped one in each hand and still they didn't fit. "Valentina," he groaned as he shifted forward to taste them, taking one delicious nipple, then the other, into his mouth.

She steadied herself on his shoulders and began moving up and down on him, slowly, deliberately, drawing her pleasure from his cock inch by inch. The feel of being inside her...sublime...*right*. Never had it felt like this.

His hands again found her hips, and he began thrusting with calculated intention. That he would reach climax was a foregone conclusion. But he wanted to bring her over that edge with him.

"You're so big," she gasped. "And you feel so good."

A chuckle rumbled from him. "Flattery will get you everywhere."

"As long as it's with you."

Her hips swiveled, grinding her quim against him, driving him wild for her, as he thrust deeper.

"You're almost too much," she gasped. A little smile hovered at the corner of her mouth. *"Almost."*

Beneath hands that nearly spanned her waist, he felt a tension enter her body—the specific tension that preceded climax. She was so...so...so close... Then on a cry that filled the carriage, she broke, her quim pulsing around him. Her head fallen to his shoulder, her breath ragged and hot against his neck, as he drove inside her, his own release building, ready to collapse on him. Then climax crashed through him, pushing him over the edge into oblivion, lighting sparks of desire, pleasure, and lust into a full conflagration. "Valentina," he shouted.

The feel of her—her body enervated and draped atop him...her slick warmth holding him tight—this was heaven. It was that simple.

At last, he slowed to a stop, panting into her hair.

Though this had been a romp in a carriage, the moment between them felt more than intimate. It felt...

Significant.

That was the difference between being with Valentina and anyone else.

With her, this act of coupling contained significance.

And perhaps it was that feeling which sent a question falling from his mouth, into her ear. "Did you mean it?" he asked with an utter seriousness that felt new. Why did everything feel new with Valentina?

"Mean what?" she asked as if the response had been dragged from her. She was still floating in the hazy, in-between state of entering her body again. From the sound of it, she was resisting.

Still, he needed to know. "What you said."

He felt a lazy smile against his neck. "I said a great many things."

As long as it's with you.

Those had been her exact words.

And he wanted to know if she'd meant them.

They'd been like an arrow shot—whissing through the air and meeting their end at a point directly in the center of his chest.

But his nerve failed him at the last second. "That part about me being so, ahem..."

"*Big?*" She giggled.

113

"*Good,*" he finished on a chuckle. "Hoyden," he added.

That would have to do for now.

He wasn't even sure he had the right to ask about the other words. After tomorrow, he may never see her again, and those were simply the words one spoke while in the throes of passion. They tended to lose their heat once bodies cooled.

Right.

"We never did get those stockings removed," he said.

She pushed against his chest and straightened, tugging her bodice up so her glorious breasts were lost to view.

He experienced a pang. This was the beginning of her separating from him.

This pang... Another novel experience.

"I believe we managed to work around them." She pushed off him, her skirts falling to her ankles before she returned to the opposite bench. He adjusted himself and closed the fall of his trousers.

As he stared across the distance now separating them, that pang stole through him again. He wanted her in his arms. He wasn't sure he'd ever let her go.

But he must. He wasn't a medieval warlord, and she wasn't truly his to claim and possess.

Right.

Toward that end, he said, "Shall we run through what will happen tonight?"

She nodded.

"There will be a point in the evening where you and I will be seen talking by Nestor. Then I will very pointedly turn in his direction and nod at him."

"Ah, The Nod." She looked slightly skeptical.

"Yes."

"And that is all?"

"When he arrives home from the musicale, a note will be waiting for him. It will inform him that he will need to be at Epsom at one of the clock tomorrow with the money in guineas."

"You think it will meet with success?"

"Yes." Archie hadn't a single doubt.

"Why?"

"Because I'm offering Nestor what he truly wants."

"Which is?"

"His family's return to the highest level of Society."

Valentina's jaw tightened. "He doesn't deserve it."

"It will be paradise regained, then paradise lost again."

"Good." She released a long exhale. "And I'm to be the silent contessa again tonight."

"Your last performance."

Her hands fidgeted with each other. "And after tomorrow, we'll have no reason to see each other again."

"Not unless you can think of one."

The words hung in the space between them, true and immovable. He hadn't spoken them with suggestion or salaciousness.

Her gaze, serious and questioning, searched his, then skittered away to stare out the window. They'd entered the City of London and would be arriving at Casa Windermere within minutes.

Archie couldn't help feeling that an opportunity was slipping away from him, if it wasn't entirely lost already.

But how to grab hold and seize it?

He hadn't experience with that.

But he would need to be a quick learner if he was to have any chance.

Chapter Thirteen

Evening

VALENTINA'S HEAD POKED out of the open carriage door and glanced about a Grosvenor Square gone dusky with encroaching night.

Happy violin music swept across her, alongside the chatter of a hundred or so guests. Her gaze lifted up and up and up the Duke and Duchess of Ripon's mansion with its Palladian colonnade of white pillars framing front doors flung wide to arriving guests.

So, this was a duke's London residence.

A sense of who the Windermeres were within London Society was only now beginning to sink in. They were wild and kind, but they held immense wealth and power, too.

Behind Delilah and Juliet, Valentina took the hand of an impassive footman and descended to cobblestones that glistened from a recent wash. Apparently, dukes cleaned, and possibly polished, their cobblestones—well, they had others do it, of course.

As she ascended front steps lit by opposing rows of candelabras, she reminded herself to breathe, even as her palms threatened to perspire through her borrowed white satin gloves. It was all simply so grand and opulent and overwhelming. Bouquets and boughs of summer roses invited guests inside with their fragrance.

Just inside the door, a servant offered to take her evening cape—rather, Juliet's—leaving Valentina clad in an evening gown of coral silk, shaped to her every curve. Her shoulders had never been so bare in public. She'd protested that the ensemble was too fine, but Juliet had insisted that it was perfect for her and wouldn't hear of having it returned.

But now, standing inside a duke's mansion, nerves jangling through her, Valentina was glad for the dress. Without it, she would have stood out as an oddity. Everyone around her—lords and ladies, earls and countesses, dukes and duchesses, kings and queens for all she knew—was decked out in their finest silks and most sparkling jewels.

Delilah tossed a questioning glance over her shoulder as they stood in the receiving line, awaiting their turn to be greeted by the Duke and Duchess.

Valentina smiled—though it may have wobbled a bit—and nodded.

"How are you faring?" asked Delilah, a spark of concern in her eyes. "I know they're a duke and duchess, but really, it's only Tristan and Amelia. She'll try to mother you—don't let her—and he might grunt at you. A man of few words, to say the least."

Juliet reached over and gave Valentina's hand a quick, reassuring squeeze. She was most grateful for Delilah and Juliet. She was also thankful that she wasn't expected to speak for the entire night, which shouldn't be an issue as Delilah and Juliet had volunteered to steer her clear of all Italians who might be in attendance. Delilah had said it would be a lark.

The Windermeres and their larks.

Apparently, they'd spent several months in Italy, riding out a scandal that had something to do with Delilah, Archie, and Eton College. They'd been fuzzy on the details, though Delilah had grumbled something about Ravensworth beneath her breath. Not that Valentina had any idea who or what a Ravensworth was.

The line before Valentina suddenly cleared, and Delilah and Juliet were to either side of her, each taking an arm and walking her forward. In a few short steps, they stood before a man and woman—he massive and handsome and she tall and possessed of the signature Windermere blonde gorgeousness. Without a doubt the Duke and Duchess of Ripon.

A more gorgeous couple Valentina had never seen. And judging by the bump in the Duchess's dress, it appeared they would be adding a gorgeous child to their family in the coming months.

"Contessa," said Delilah with a wink, "meet the Duke and Duchess of Ripon."

Valentina dipped into a shallow curtsy. Or what passed for one, she supposed. She'd never been required to curtsy in all her life. Of course, she'd never met such personages in all her life who would require a curtsy. Small, but important distinction.

The Duke nodded and... Was that a grunt?

The Duchess stepped forward and took one of Valentina's hands with a welcoming smile. "I hear you're to sing for us tonight, *Contessa*," she said. She didn't wink like Delilah, but a twinkle certainly shone in her eyes.

"*Si*," said Valentina, clutching the handle of her bag tighter. Instead of carrying a dainty reticule like all the other ladies in attendance, she carried a folio case filled with sheet music.

Earlier this evening, when Delilah and Juliet had been helping her get ready, Delilah had asked where she'd met Archie. In a moment of distraction—for Tucker had become quite intent on wrangling the delicate silk bodice higher above her too-bounteous bosom, having, at last, to settle for a fichu for modesty—Valentina said, "The Five Graces."

A look passed between Delilah and Juliet. A look that said she'd just confirmed their suspicions. "So, it was *you*," said Delilah.

"*Me?*"

"Who we've heard singing in the night," said Juliet.

Ah. "Erm, yes."

Delilah clapped with delight. "You must sing at the musicale tonight."

"Why?"

"Whyever not?"

If the Windermeres had a mantra, that would be it. *Whyever not.*

"You have talent," said Juliet.

Valentina saw no choice available to her but to agree.

"I'll inform Amelia to add you to the performance list," said Delilah.

"As the final performer," added Juliet. "She'll be the best."

After Delilah and Juliet left to finish their own preparations, Valentina had a moment to think, and in an instant, a decision came to her. She might be displaying her talent tonight for all the aristocracy...

But she wouldn't be doing it alone.

So, she'd slipped into Archie's bedroom and taken a few sheets of music. The Mozart she would need, and another, too.

Now, she gripped the case tightly. She'd refused to let a servant take it with her cape. Its cargo was too precious to let out of her sight. If everyone thought her an eccentric Italian contessa for carrying it, let them.

As she walked with Delilah and Juliet through the spacious mansion bedecked in all manner of sculptures and paintings, fine woods and marbles, again a sense of awe threatened to overwhelm her. She was a guest at a duke and duchess's musicale. She didn't think she would be telling her family. Mama wouldn't approve, as she disapproved of aristocrats in the general sense.

Actually, that wasn't entirely true.

After their meal this afternoon—was it only eight hours ago?—she'd caught Mama gazing upon Archie with an expression suspiciously close to approval.

And the thing was Archie hadn't been his usual, overly charming self. He'd been relaxed and showed genuine curiosity about the lives of her family. In the end, she'd felt strangely proud to have brought him to meet them. Though she suspected she would suffer endless rounds of teasing from her brothers about,

"That time Valentina brought a nob to Sunday tea."

Speaking of...

Where was the nob she'd brought to Sunday tea?

She glanced around the room they were passing through. *Room* was too humble a word for this space with its gleaming mahogany floors and crystal chandeliers, which threw golden light onto every surface—be it marble tabletop, a mustache curved into a laugh, or a bare ivory shoulder caught in an ironic shrug. Where she strolled with Delilah and Juliet guests mingled comfortably, while at the opposite end of the room chairs were assembled into straight rows for the musical portion of the evening.

It was a lovely, cultured gathering; everything and everyone proper and in their place. Even so, Valentina thought she might prefer the loose raucous gatherings in Hampstead's small assembly rooms. What they lacked in perfection, they made up for in fun—a concept with which much of the population of this room didn't seem to be acquainted. Not like...

Archie.

Another scan of the room found no sign of him, but she'd known it before she'd looked. The composition of the air would be different were he here.

She hadn't seen him since they'd arrived back at Casa Windermere in the late afternoon. Not since they'd...oh, they'd... Her body heated a few degrees... Not since their—oh, there was no better word for it, so help her—*romp* in his carriage.

This afternoon combined with last night... A possibility occurred to her.

She might be mad for Archie.

How else could she countenance her shameless behavior?

"You look a trifle flushed, Valentina," said Juliet.

"Shall we deposit you in a quiet corner and fetch you a cup of punch?" asked Delilah, already escorting Valentina to said quiet corner. "There are even curtains you can hide behind if the situation gets sticky."

"In fact, you might want to anyway," said Juliet. "I've noted no fewer than five lords risking neck spasms while trying to get a better look at you."

Delilah and Juliet deposited Valentina in the discreet corner and set to their task. She felt better here than she had since entering this mansion. The people milling about this room weren't her people.

Then she felt *it*…

Archie's presence.

She shifted, so she could see properly around the curtain, and swept her gaze over the room. Her eyes landed on a pair of men just entering—one short and frowning; the other tall and golden and blithely smiling, utterly and completely in his element, dressed in evening blacks. No few glances stole his way. Archie was simply that magnetic.

Valentina forgot to breathe as his gaze shifted and discreetly scanned the room, slowly making his way toward…*her*. Their eyes locked, and the distance between them turned to nothing. It was only he and she in this too-grand room. The smile on his mouth fell not an increment, but the one in his eyes deepened as he gave her a slow, thorough up-and-down, taking in her evening finery.

A bold thought came to her.

He would like what he saw with her every curve on display.

Except the fichu.

He wouldn't like that.

In the next tick of time, his gaze returned to the man at his side—Lord Nestor. They exchanged a few words with Nestor's gaze flicking toward Valentina. Then Archie began walking. Toward her. Though not in a straight line. Every few steps, he was accosted by a different acquaintance or friend or even family member, for all she knew. It was widely known that most aristocrats were related either through blood or marriage or, more than occasionally, both. And all the while, his too-charming smile didn't slip a whit. This was Lord Daniel Windermere,

Viscount Archer—*Archie*—in his natural element. Yet...

His gaze never strayed from her for longer than a few seconds at a time.

The other guests might receive his charm, but she held the entirety of his attention.

She rather liked that.

Too much.

He only stopped when he'd come within three feet of her. Silence stretched between them. There was simply too much to say.

"Smile," he said at last.

"Pardon?"

"For Nestor."

And she understood. The ruse was on. A too-large smile stretched across her mouth. All the muscles in her face would be sore in the morning if she kept this up for longer than two minutes.

"Now, pretend we're talking."

"We are talking," she couldn't help pointing out.

A hint of his true smile shone in his eyes. "Are you..." he began. "Are you being treated well?"

She nodded. "Your family is most kind."

"Are you thirsty?"

"Delilah and Juliet are fetching me a cup of punch."

He laughed as if she'd told the funniest joke in the world. "Now you laugh," he said.

She laughed, knowing it was for Nestor.

"Have you eaten?" asked Archie.

"I'm not hungry, my lord," she said. "And you?"

"What about me?"

"Did you eat your fill this afternoon?"

He went stone still, the only movement on his body the flare of black pupils pushing blue irises into thin rings. Of a sudden, her question wasn't about Sunday tea with her family.

Had she intended it that way?

She thought not, but…perhaps…

Hoyden.

"I'll never have my fill of that particular meal," he said, shimmering with the dark intensity that so attracted her.

A shiver purled up her spine and crawled through her body, tightening her nipples, making her ready for him. The pleasures he'd introduced to her body, she wanted more of them. *Now.*

Which was, of course, impossible.

"Now for The Nod," he said.

She did as instructed. She would do anything he asked, she suspected—and feared.

He tore his gaze from her and nodded at Lord Nestor. He nodded back.

The swindle of the swindler was on.

Archie stepped forward, and Valentina's heart skipped into a race. "Valentina, about last night…"

"Yes?"

"And this afternoon…"

"Yes?"

Why was her heart suddenly in her throat?

"I may not have been at my best," he said.

She held his gaze for a full five seconds before a burst of laughter that might have been slightly hysterical broke from her. "That wasn't your best?"

To Archie's credit, he did try to remain serious, but the smile that wanted out wouldn't be stifled. "Blast it, woman, you know what I mean. I'm trying to apologize for being no more than a rake. I've had time to think about it."

Pique needled through Valentina. "But here's the thing, Lord Archer," she said. "*I'm* not apologizing to *you.*"

"Pardon?"

"What we experienced together was mutual. I made the desired decision for myself, and you made the desired decision for yourself. I believe we each reached the desired outcome."

Archie's mouth opened, then closed. The man was thoroughly nonplussed. She felt no small amount of satisfaction.

The *ding-ding-ding* of metal tapping crystal sounded at the opposite end of the room. The Duke and Duchess of Ripon stood in the center aisle of the assembled rows of chairs. "If you will make your way to a chair, the musical portion of the evening will begin." Every syllable sounded as if extracted with great reluctance from His Grace, while Her Grace stood serenely by his side.

Archie didn't seem to have heard, for he yet stared down at Valentina, his head cocked, his gaze gone narrow and assessing, as if he were running a mental calculation.

"I believe this is when you escort me to my chair, my lord," she said.

"Our work for the night is finished," he said, low. "We could leave and no one would be the wiser."

He didn't need to speak the words aloud for her body to know precisely what he was suggesting. They could leave...*together.*

Then she felt it in her hand. The folio case.

"We are expected to stay," she said, summoning every bit of will she possessed, for the plain fact was she wouldn't mind taking him up on his unspoken suggestion.

Disappointment flashed behind his eyes. Then he held out an arm for her, and they made their way through the crowd to the front row of seats that Delilah and Juliet had saved for them.

"Did you have to sit us all the way at the front, Delilah?" Archie groused.

"Yes," she said simply.

Nerves filled Valentina. Archie only thought his work finished for the evening.

The Duke and Duchess took their seats to the other side of Delilah and Juliet, and the musicale began. It quickly became clear the musical entertainments provided by a duke and duchess couldn't be more different from those provided by the Five Graces. There, the evening would've begun with a contortionist or a puppet act. Here, two rather burly footmen were hauling out a full-sized, gilded harp. A lady, whose attire was fashioned in the manner of an ancient Grecian statue, took her seat and began plucking the strings, the music flowing over the assembled like a gentle stream.

Valentina stole a glance at Archie. Where she felt relaxed by the music, his hands were clenched at his sides and his gaze steadfastly fixed on the harpist. She immediately understood. For Archie, music wasn't a recreational experience to be enjoyed and forgotten. It entered his body and fused with his soul. It was no less dramatic than that, she sensed.

The harpist played three pieces, curtsied, and left alongside her massive gilt instrument. Next, a piano was rolled into its place, and a woman who could be none other than an opera singer stood before the gathering in a dramatic velvet crimson cloak and set her gaze toward an indistinct point in the distance, waiting, while a slight man took his place at the piano. Archie remained utterly transfixed when the singer launched into Bach's *"Ich esse mit Freuden."*

The mezzosoprano's voice burst into life and filled every corner, and all Valentina could do was sit back in awe of her virtuosity. This woman's voice had been trained by professionals.

And she was to follow her?

Valentina understood she possessed a lovely voice, but it was untrained. Well, there was nothing for it. She had a plan of her own tonight, and she would see it through.

It struck her that she was about to sing for aristocrats, as she'd originally intended. But tonight, instead of exposing Lord Nestor, she would be exposing Archie. Perhaps it was wrong, but deep in her soul, she felt its rightness.

Her soul knew something about Archie's, and it understood it needed to see the light.

Or the darkness would consume him.

The mezzosoprano sang through several more Bach pieces before finishing her musical set. The crowd clapped politely. Valentina shook her head. *Aristocrats.* They'd witnessed true vocal virtuosity, and they seemed slightly bored—all except for the man beside her.

The Duchess of Ripon leaned forward and nodded at Valentina. It was time.

She removed the sheet music from the folio case and stood, sudden anxiety jittering through her, giving her hands a slight tremor. Beside her, Archie's eyebrows crinkled together in question.

She took her place in the bentside curve of the piano and gazed out across the crowd of one hundred slightly indifferent pairs of eyes. She swallowed and found the only pair of eyes that mattered. Then she crooked her finger.

He gave his head a subtle shake.

She smiled, unmoved. She'd anticipated as much.

He must've reached the—correct—conclusion that she would stand here all night if necessary, for finally he stood. A few gasps rippled through the crowd, and interest in the night's musicale perked up.

Archie smiled his charming smile, but the stormy look in his eyes was all for Valentina. He was none too pleased with her.

No matter.

As he seated himself on the bench, she placed the Mozart piece onto the music stand before him. Their eyes caught for a quick instant. She would be explaining herself later, his eyes told her. Oh, if he only knew…

His fingers depressed keys, and the opening notes of Mozart's *"Voi che sapete"* lifted into the air, *pianissimo*, so as not to overwhelm her voice when she began singing. Again, they met eye to eye, as musicians, and they made music together. At first, he resisted entering the emotion of the piece with her, trying to be naught more than an accompanist, but she saw the instant he gave over. He couldn't help himself. He could give nothing less than his all to music. It inspired Valentina's voice to new heights as she gave her all to Mozart.

Too soon, the final notes poured from her and sounded from the piano. The crowd erupted into applause, with Delilah shouting, *"Bravissimo!"*

Archie made to stand. He'd only reached a half crouch before

Valentina shook her head. She pulled another piece of music from the folio case and placed it before him. His gaze swiped over it, and his jaw tightened. His eyes met hers, and he shook his head.

She nodded.

He shook his head again.

Their audience laughed, assuming Archie was only being his usual Windermere self. What new jape had he in store for them?

Valentina had come prepared for this moment.

She pulled a slip of paper from the folio case and slid it across the gleaming rosewood fallboard. He scanned the two simple words.

I'll speak.

It was a gamble. He could easily call her bluff. But she felt he wouldn't. It would ruin tomorrow's plan for Nestor, and Archie wouldn't let that opportunity slip by.

A muscle in his jaw jumped, but that was the only outward sign of his anger as the first notes of the composition—*his* composition—fell from his fingertips. She could have picked any one of his thirty two compositions, but she'd chosen this one—the one they'd created together.

She stepped away from the piano and returned to her seat in the front row. She wanted to watch his performance along with everyone else.

He began the piece slowly, so it sounded almost like a dirge, but despite himself, he entered the music. As he played, it was only him and the music, and everyone in the room sensed it, even if they didn't fully understand it. How was this the Viscount Archer playing *that* music? Skilled fingers flew across the keyboard, displaying his mastery of the instrument. Even if the room didn't know the beautiful music pouring from his soul was his own composition, they witnessed his command and skill.

Valentina had never seen him more gorgeous than he was at this moment—the composition building on itself, gathering intensity, casting a spell over the room. She would wager not a single breath was drawn during the entirety of the performance.

Then the final notes echoed out and faded. Three beats of

silence held before the assembled burst into rapturous applause.

Archie stood and gave a bow, his mouth held in the tight approximation of a smile, a far cry from the usual devil-may-care one all knew well.

All Valentina saw was thinly veiled fury.

He stepped away from the instrument and made for the front row...

For *her*.

He stopped inches from her and held out a hand. "You're coming with me," he said, low and utterly, entirely intent.

"Now Archie—" began Delilah.

He shot his sister a silencing look. "This has nothing to do with you, Delilah."

Her mouth snapped shut.

"We'll cause a scene," said Valentina.

And he smiled. Valentina didn't like that smile. It held a menacing quality. "Oh, it's nothing to the scene we'll cause if you don't come with me *now*."

And that was how Valentina found herself arm in arm with Archie, being marched down the central aisle, curious, shocked stares and mutterings being thrown their way as they exited the mansion through the open set of double doors. As they strode into a moonlit garden, he remained silent. His pace didn't abate as they followed one gravel path, then another, through shrubberies and rows of fruit trees, the garden growing more enchanting with every step away from the mansion and its music and the crowd's chatter growing fainter. This garden was in the middle of London?

They stepped inside a walled-off portion, all grown over with vines and climbing roses. A secret garden, lit by small hanging globes. But she hadn't time to stare in appreciation for she had a furious lord to contend with.

Archie dropped her arm and placed some distance between them before pivoting. This man had something to say to her.

Which was just as well.

She had something to say to him.

"Apologize," he said—*demanded*.

She should've known he'd be capable of this sort of fury, but it still came as a shock. "I don't believe I shall."

She had some ground to stand, and she would.

His eyebrows lifted in perplexity.

She'd surprised him.

Good.

He cocked his head. "Do you think what you did was right?"

It was a genuine question. She would give him a genuine answer. "I'm not certain. But I do know one thing."

"What's that?"

"You need to stop being a fake."

There, she'd said it.

"A fake?" An incredulous laugh escaped him. "You're the one pretending to be an Italian contessa."

She shook her head. "The two are not at all the same, and you know it."

His jaw clenched, and the thunderstorm returned to his eyes. He couldn't deny it.

Here, Valentina found the opening she needed. "You have two selves."

"You make me sound like a bedlamite," he said, as lordly and dismissive as she'd ever heard him. She'd definitely struck a nerve.

"The Lord Archer that the world knows, and this other man only revealed in the dead of night," she began. "I don't understand why it's so necessary to keep them separate."

He looked as if he wouldn't respond, then he said, "Everyone loves the Lord Archer they know. He's always up for a lark and a laugh." He shrugged, as if indifferent. "Does the world really need another temperamental artist?"

She didn't hesitate. "Yes."

"Why is that, pray tell?"

"So you can stop living half a life."

Chapter Fourteen

Archie went stone still, as if mere words could bind one physically.

But her words weren't mere.

They had the power to clear all the fury from his body in an instant.

He felt…

Seen.

And for the first time in his life he experienced permission to feel that way.

Because it was this woman who saw him.

Valentina.

He propped a shoulder against a bare patch of garden wall and crossed his arms over his chest. "Do you want to know something, Valentina?"

Her eyes narrowed with sudden wariness. "What?"

She didn't trust the smile now curling about his mouth. Perhaps she was right not to. His smile set hidden places inside her aflame—he'd noticed.

"You're incredibly beautiful when you're scolding me."

Her mouth clamped shut, and though it was difficult to tell in the monochrome light of the moon, he thought her cheeks might have brightened into a dusky pink blush.

The next instant, she collected herself. She wasn't finished. "You think you can't be vulnerable, so you hide behind that gorgeous smile of yours."

Oh, what he was about to ask next was really going to infuriate her. "You think my smile is gorgeous?"

She let out a near growl of frustration. "The *ton* will still like you. The *whole* you."

He could love her for her earnestness.

Could...love?

The idea, novel and not unappealing, stunned him.

A thought for later, perhaps.

She needed to understand something, now. "I like to be liked in the general sense." He shrugged. "It's rather nice that I elicit that response in people. But I don't particularly give a toss whether or not the people in that mansion"—he pointed toward Tristan and Amelia's impressive residence—"like all of me, or even half of me." He pushed off the wall. "I care about the opinion of only one person."

She swallowed. "And who is that?" she asked, a telling rasp in her voice.

"Do you like me?"

"Yes...sometimes."

He spread his hands wide. "See? Even you prefer one Archie over the other."

She shook her head, her eyes burning, and closed the distance between them. He just caught a hint of her familiar lemon and rose scent. "I like the Archie who expresses himself from *here*." Her forefinger dug into his chest. "From the heart."

Before he could think about what he was doing, he caught her hand and peeled the glove away. He brought her hand to his mouth. Her skin against his, even this small patch, the dose that only enhanced need. For it was a fact he'd become addicted to her. On instinct, his mouth trailed to her wrist. "And do you like the Archie who kisses you *here*?"

"Yes," she said, a bit breathless, her luminous amber eyes

gone cloudy with tell-tale desire.

He inched closer, trailing up the sensitive skin of her inner arm, leaving goose bumps in his wake. She steadied herself with her other hand on his shoulder.

He'd made her knees go weak.

He liked that.

What he was doing at this moment... What he was contemplating doing in the next few moments... It was madness.

That was the long and short of it.

He was absolutely mad for this woman.

So mad he would take her in a duke's secret garden, if she would have him.

He reached the delicate sleeve of her coral silk gown, whose color sat perfectly against her olive complexion. He wanted to taste the delicate line of her clavicle, but there was something he must do first. "Can I please toss this horrid fichu into the bushes?"

She breathed out a laugh. "Yes."

"Who thought it was a good idea to conceal these curves?" he asked, untucking the offending garment and flinging it away. "They must be celebrated and worshipped." He ran his tongue along her collarbone before dipping to kiss one creamy mound, then the other, appreciating that this dress was barely up to the task of containing them.

A voice of reason cut through the fog of desire.

He should retrieve her fichu and stop here.

Digging deep inside himself and summoning every last ounce of will, he straightened, thereby removing his mouth from her body.

Valentina's eyes flew open. "What are you doing?"

"What I should have done last night." A beat. "And this afternoon." Another beat. "And thirty seconds ago." He swallowed against his dry throat. "I'm being a gentleman and stopping," he said, hoarse.

"*Stopping?*" she asked, incredulous. She reached out and grabbed his cravat. "And what if I have no interest in being a lady?"

The thing was, he'd never possessed strength of will when it came to resisting pleasures of the flesh.

And resisting the pleasure that was Miss Valentina Hart? *Impossible.*

She sensed his relenting the instant he did. She tugged him forward by the cravat and met his mouth with hers, their hands suddenly hungry for each other. All that was pent up between them released.

All the need and all the want...

All the passion and all the desire.

She'd pushed his evening coat off his shoulders, and he had her shawl discarded. As she peeled off her other glove, he took her waist in his hands and walked her backward. Then he had her pressed against the garden wall. She had his waistcoat unbuttoned and sliding off his shoulders, and he had her bodice open, her full breasts peaking beneath her chemise. Through diaphanous muslin, his mouth found a nipple firm and sweet as a cherry in summer. Her hands were frantically untucking his shirt from the waistband of his trousers.

Even as he was pulling the shirt over his head, he said, "You know it isn't necessary to remove my shirt for the consummation of this act."

Her nakedly appreciative gaze raked over his bare chest. "Oh, yes, it is."

He chuckled, the laugh gravel against his throat. She wanted him, desperately, as she leaned against the wall, her body languorous and waiting to be taken by him. His cock strained against his trousers. Who was he to keep a lady waiting?

He grabbed her skirts, and she slid one shapely leg around his waist, her arms around his neck, as their bodies strained against each other. Her sex open to him, his hard cock grazed against her, only the superfine of his trousers keeping them apart. She swiveled her hips, grinding against him, and exhaled a soft, "Oh," into his mouth.

Her hands trailed down his chest, savoring the feel of his skin. She sent electricity sparking through him, his body anticipating the downward trajectory of her fingers. He waited as they caressed chest, stomach—muscles involuntarily bunching beneath her touch—and reached the fall of his trousers, releasing his ready cock with a few quick movements. Then it was skin against skin, the slick heat of her quim soft against his hard, rigid length that throbbed and ached for her.

Lust-glazed eyes caught his from beneath thick lashes. "I need you, Archie, so..." He grazed against the entrance of her sex. "...so fiercely," she uttered, tightening her leg around him, bringing their bodies closer, bringing him into her. He took her hips in hand so it was a slow, deliberate thrust.

Then he was where he should be.

Inside her.

One with her.

She groaned, even whimpered, against his neck as he stroked in and out of her, measured, relentless, her back against the garden wall, her head angled to the side in abandon. What he was delivering to her body with each and every thrust she had to have—she couldn't live without.

As long as it's with you.

Those words echoed through him as he took her. They'd entered and created a space within him that only she filled. And this act of coupling only intensified the feeling—a feeling he understood in the deepest part of himself he would only experience with her.

A tryst against a garden wall was supposed to be a frenzied, naughty coupling. But *this*—what he felt with her—wasn't *that*—a diversion that would be forgotten almost as quickly as it was finished.

This...with her...he wanted it to last.

He slowed his movements and entered her with intention. She would feel him, and not just his cock. *Him.*

She ground against him and released a sigh, her sex opening

further, giving him all.

"Valentina," he rumbled low in her ear. "Open your eyes."

Her gaze slitted open and found his. What he met there—desire, but something more, too…a responding depth of emotion—nearly stole his breath. Was it possible he wasn't alone in his feelings?

A bead of sweat trailed down her neck, and he caught it with his tongue. Her hand tightened on his shoulder, and she thrust against him, hard. She wanted *more*, and he would give it to her.

Then, too soon, the promise—the threat—of release was pressing down on them. Mindless with pleasure, her nails clawed down his back. He steadied and thrust inside her, stroke after unrelenting stroke, giving her what they both needed. Then she was crying out, her sex pulsing its release around him, and he was pouring his climax into her. Together, they tumbled into the sweet abyss that transcended the bonds of earth.

Their hearts raced as one; the ragged, unified rhythm of their breath the garden's only sound, his body pressed against her, her sole support against the wall.

Only she existed here with him.

In the entire universe, only she, in his arms, mattered.

But, slowly, inevitably, a separation occurred as they reentered themselves, no longer one. He slid from her. "Can you stand?"

She nodded, looking uncertain even so.

He pulled away and tried not to stare at this woman replete and gorgeous with satiety, lips swollen and kiss-crushed, body flushed with pleasure delivered.

He could take her again.

Now.

But he wouldn't. They'd already been pushing their luck with a single tryst. Twice would be utterly irresponsible. It wouldn't be his reputation that suffered, but hers, if they were found out. He wouldn't subject Valentina to that shame.

He began to dress, as did she, silence stretching between

them. When he finally knotted his cravat and put the finishing touches on his hasty toilette, he faced her. She was dressed, but she looked slightly...*askew*.

"Let me..." He closed the few feet between them. "I have sisters."

Efficiently, he set to work straightening her out—untwisting her bodice, brushing the wrinkles from her skirts with his hand, plucking an ivy leaf from her hair. "There," he said, at last, stepping back and surveying his handiwork. Still, something felt off or missing, and he couldn't quite grasp what it was.

"So," she began and stopped. She looked suddenly shy of him.

Too late for that.

"So," he responded.

Like a dolt.

She looked as if she were building up to say something more, and finally she did. "How do you make me so wild for you, Archie?"

"That isn't *me*, Valentina." He needed her to understand. "It's *us*."

He had more to say to this woman.

Too much more.

Which was the problem.

Where to start?

It was she who started without him. "About tomorrow."

"Yes?" he asked, impatient. He didn't want to talk about tomorrow. He wanted to talk about the here and now before it drifted away into the night and was lost to them.

"Nestor has the money?"

"Yes." He didn't want to talk about money, either.

He wanted to talk about this feeling currently clogging his chest and making it impossible for him to breathe properly.

"Then it will be done," she said.

"And once it's done?" he asked.

She blinked.

This was what he wanted to talk about. "We could have an

136

arrangement."

Her brow crinkled. "An arrangement?"

"Where we keep seeing each other."

"As lovers?"

He nodded, even as a feeling crept in that this was turning down a *wrong, wrong, wrong* path.

But he was powerless to stop the momentum.

She shook her head. "That won't be possible."

"I think you'll find it's very much within the realm of possibility." He took a step forward, as if closing the physical distance between them would also close the widening emotional gap. "I'm mad for you, Valentina. You must know that. You're my obsession."

The question in her eyes cleared. *"Ah."*

"Ah?" He didn't like the sound of her *ah*. It wasn't at all like the other *ahs* he'd been pulling from her minutes ago.

"And your obsessions must be kept secret, mustn't they?"

How had it all spiraled out of his control so quickly?

She wasn't finished. "An *arrangement* would put me beyond the pale with my family, and that isn't something I'm willing to risk. Not even for you, Archie."

And he knew.

He'd gone about this all wrong.

And he knew how.

He'd asked her the wrong question.

"Oh," sounded a familiar voice, "there you two are."

Archie and Valentina's heads whipped around to find Delilah and Juliet entering the secret garden. For a few beats of time too long, they four stared at each other in silence. Though his sister and cousin were innocents, they weren't fools. They understood at once something had just occurred between him and Valentina. The knowledge shone plain in their eyes.

The instant after Juliet's gaze caught on a diaphanous white patch in the shrubberies, so did everyone else's. Archie could kick himself. *That* was what had been missing from Valentina's hurried toilette. *The fichu.*

Juliet untangled it from a tenacious limb and handed it to Valentina in discreet silence. Delilah's chin notched up a full inch, her eyes gone hard. "Archie, I think it's time for you to leave."

He nodded. He deserved as much. Reflexively, he held out his arm to Valentina.

"Valentina stays with us," said Juliet.

Right. That was him told.

Delilah and Juliet had closed ranks around Valentina, and he couldn't deny that they were correct to do so.

He gave a bow that was equal parts irony and anger, pivoted on his heel, and strode from the secret garden toward the mansion. With each footstep, fury collected within him and settled deep inside his gut—a fury that was directed squarely at one person.

Himself.

He'd botched matters with Valentina, utterly and irrevocably.

Fool.

He entered the mansion, meaning to say his farewells to Tristan and Amelia, with whom he hadn't yet spoken with this evening, but he'd taken no more than five steps inside when he heard a familiar voice at his back, "There you are."

He inhaled a calming breath before pivoting to find one of his oldest friends in the world, His Grace Sebastian Crewe, the Duke of Ravensworth, watching him with a slightly lifted brow and his usual sardonic smile. While Ravensworth matched Archie for height, standing a few inches over six feet tall, he was bulkier in the way gentlemen who took boxing as their exercise were. And where Archie's hair shone at the platinum end of blond, Ravensworth's was a few shades darker.

"Ravensworth," said Archie.

His friend cut directly to it. "The opera singer... I'm not acquainted with her."

"I've never seen her," said Archie, in a hurry. "You'll have to ask Amelia for her direction."

Ravensworth's smile reached his eyes, a rarity. "Not that opera singer. The other one."

The breath froze in Archie's chest. Ravensworth had noticed Valentina. Of course, Ravensworth had noticed Valentina. The man was a known patron of the arts—his name was on half a dozen buildings throughout England and the Continent. But that wouldn't be the only reason he'd noticed her.

It was all Archie could do not to clench his fists at his sides.

"*La Contessa,*" he said. He'd be damned if he offered Ravensworth her real name.

"Do you know if she's in need of a patronage?" asked Ravensworth. Either he hadn't noticed Archie's increasingly foul mood, or he'd noticed and simply didn't give a toss. Ravensworth could be very much a duke in that way.

"She's a contessa," said Archie, digging in. "Why would she need your patronage?"

Ravensworth scoffed. "Come off it. She's no more a contessa than you are a stonemason."

It would be pointless to try to convince Ravensworth otherwise. The man was too astute for that—and he knew Archie too well.

He dug into his breast pocket, his hand emerging with a white slip of paper. "Give this to her." He extended a calling card toward Archie. "My door is always open for talent such as hers."

A tidal wave of jealousy washed over Archie. There was simply no stopping it. "I'm sure it's her talent you noticed," he nearly growled.

Ravensworth's light amber eyes narrowed, and he went cold in that way particular to him. "You insult her talent, Arch." He inclined his head. "I'll bid you a good night."

Archie decided it wasn't in him to make small talk with Tristan and Amelia. It was time to leave.

He took the front steps leading onto Grosvenor Square down two at a time. Only when he was a good half mile away did his racing mind begin to slow and form a few clear thoughts.

He'd revealed something of his feelings about Valentina to Ravensworth—feelings he hadn't quite sorted through himself.

But that wasn't what irritated him most about the interaction. The man had been correct. He *had* insulted Valentina's talent. The truth was the patronage of the Duke of Ravensworth would ensure an illustrious career for her. Archie should turn around and give her the calling card this instant.

Instead, he slipped it into his breast pocket.

Tomorrow…*tomorrow.*

He needed to gather all the frayed edges of himself together and regain control before tomorrow. Tomorrow, he had a job to do for Valentina. It was imperative that he not fail her or her family.

Even if success ensured he would never see her again.

So be it.

He would see her future secured.

Even if that future wasn't with him.

Good deeds brought their own sort of punishment.

It was a fact.

Chapter Fifteen

Next day

THE OUTSKIRTS OF London rolling past the carriage window, Valentina stroked a nervous palm along Miss Hiss's fuzzy gray fur. The kitten had finally settled and curled into a tiny ball on Valentina's lap, her sharp claws serenely kneading worn wool skirts.

She didn't mind, for she was dressed in her own clothes.

She'd insisted on it.

After the coming events of the next hour, she would be moving on with her own life—not the Windermere life she'd been leading these last several days.

Archie rode into view. He'd chosen to ride alongside the carriage to Epsom, leaving her alone with the kitten in the carriage.

Alone with thoughts that kept circling her mind like a whirligig.

Of course, she was anxious about the double swindle they were about to attempt. She snorted lightly. Only Archie could come up with such a bold, mad idea. But the thing about Archie's bold, mad ideas was they possessed a certain creativity and scope that infused their madness with possibility. They were just mad enough to work.

Archie... She took him in—gorgeous in the saddle with the midday sun glinting off his golden curls. He held such calm command and assurance.

Of course, he wasn't the only mad one between them.

These last few days she'd been consumed with an utter madness for the man. *Insatiable...hoyden...* And last night, when he'd suggested an *arrangement*, she'd told him *no* when every cell in her body had wanted—*demanded*—she say *yes*. How could she give him up?

And yet...

She must. Men like him—*lords*—didn't enter into relationships with women like her—*commoners*—unless they were of the *arrangement* variety.

This infatuation...

It would pass.

That was what she would keep telling herself until it was true.

The Epsom racecourse came into view—a brown dirt track surrounding an oval of lush green grass. A few riders were out, taking their horses through their paces. Valentina had never been to a racecourse or seen horses quite like these—coats sleek and shiny, dense muscles working just beneath the skin in tension and release as they went from trot to canter to gallop.

And Lord Nestor thought he would be leaving the track with one such animal?

He was in for quite the surprise.

The carriage slowed to a gentle stop, as if careful of not disturbing Miss Hiss's slumber.

The time had arrived.

To secure her family's lost savings.

To never see Archie again.

The carriage door swung open. She expected a footman's hand to appear in the opening. Instead, Archie pushed inside and shut the door behind him. He sat on the bench opposite her and ran a hand through his hair. She knew him well enough now to understand it as a nervous gesture. She met his gaze and detected a storm in there. He'd left his usual smiling self outside.

"Are you ready?" he asked at last. She sensed that wasn't what he'd come here to say.

"No...yes," she said, waiting for the real conversation to begin.

"If it all goes sideways, you're safe. I'll keep my word."

"What do you mean?"

"I'll compensate your family, and the other families, too."

"You don't have to pay the price for another man's transgressions."

"I made a promise," he said tightly. "And I will honor it."

She let a moment pass, then asked, "Is that all you came here to say?"

She attempted to clear her mind as she waited for his response.

She wouldn't let herself hope.

He nodded. "There is something else."

Valentina's heart kicked into a gallop. No horse on the track was moving faster. "What is it?"

Archie dug into the breast pocket of his greatcoat and pulled out a white slip of paper. A calling card. He extended it across the footwell.

Ravensworth.

That was all it said.

Her eyebrows lifted in silent question.

"The Duke of Ravensworth," said Archie.

"He and I are not acquainted," she said, as if the fact weren't already obvious.

Archie's jaw tensed and released. "But you could be."

"Should I feel insulted?" She'd made her view on *arrangements* perfectly clear last night.

"Ravensworth is a known patron of the arts. His patronage would guarantee you the illustrious career you and your talent deserve."

"And what would be the price of the Duke of Ravensworth's patronage?"

Archie flinched, and Valentina felt a frisson of rotten triumph.

"I've known Ravensworth for twenty years. He's a good man."

But even as Archie spoke the words, Valentina sensed he wasn't wholly certain of them. In the eyes of other men, a man could be a "good man" *and* a cad to women. Other men would never see that side of their friend.

Valentina nodded and slipped the calling card into her reticule. Not that she had any intention of using it. The duke's patronage would only keep her in Archie's orbit, and she understood at a fundamental level that she needed to be loosed from his world to be free to find happiness without him.

Archie didn't move, but kept studying her in silence.

"Is there anything else?" she asked, her irritation showing.

"You're still not apologizing for last night?"

She shook her head. "No. I don't regret it."

"Do you have any regrets?"

"None."

Tension tightened into knots between them.

He was opening his mouth to speak when a face appeared in the window. "Papa!" Valentina exclaimed.

The carriage door opened, and the moment slipped away. Whatever Archie had been about to say, gone.

And perhaps that was for the best.

Papa's hand appeared to assist her down from the carriage. She opened her travel bag and settled Miss Hiss inside, leaving the closure open wide enough for the kitten to poke her head through. Once on the ground, Papa took Valentina in one of his huge hugs, and she allowed warmth and safety to sink into her. When they separated, she found Archie watching them with half a smile. He respected and admired her relationship with her family. She liked that about him.

Oh, she couldn't think about the things she liked about Archie.

He got directly down to business with Papa, taking charge

without becoming overbearing. He didn't demand it, but others naturally deferred to him due to his air of authenticity.

She'd been wrong when she'd called him a fake. The fact was the man contained a multitude of characteristics.

Papa nodded his agreement with the plan and took himself off to tell the others.

A coach-and-four rolled into view, and Archie caught Valentina's eye. "Ready?"

She nodded as the carriage stopped. The door swung open, and Lord Nestor descended with the assistance of a footman. Archie snorted as the coachman lugged a trunk off the back of the carriage and let it drop near Archie's feet with a clunk that jingled just a little.

A swagger in his step, Nestor made his way toward them. "Took some doing to get it all in guineas," he called out, his gaze fixed on the horses taking their paces on the track. "One of those ours?"

A smile tipped about Archie's mouth. "Funny you should mention that."

Nestor's eyebrows crinkled together. He sensed something in the air. He glanced about, a rising panic in his eyes, his jaw tensed. His gaze brushed across Valentina before whipping back around and settling on her. "You…" He was clearly having difficulty linking the woman before him with *La Contessa*. "Why are you dressed like…like…*that*."

"Like a servant?" she asked.

His expression turned to utter befuddlement. "And why are you talking like *that*?"

"Like an Englishwoman?" she asked, unable to keep a mean, little smile from curling about her mouth. Miss Hiss's attitude might've been rubbing off on her.

Nestor's eyes rounded into saucers, and his skin went from pale milk to scarlet in an instant. "Archer, where is our horse?"

"Ah, yes, of course." Archie signaled a stable lad some fifty yards away. He nodded and fetched a horse from the nearest paddock. Valentina squinted at the animal. It appeared docile and well cared for, but also old as Methuselah.

The scarlet of Nestor's skin transitioned into a ghastly shade of green. "What is this, Archer?" he sputtered.

Archie threw his arm wide. "Meet Arabian."

"*Arabian?* That is no Arabian," fumed Nestor.

"That's the old chap's name," said Archie. He tapped a contemplative finger against his mouth. "Although I think it must've been ironic."

Nestor's eyes narrowed. "Do you think to swindle me, Archer?" He barked an ugly laugh. "I'll have your reputation in tatters by nightfall. More than a few members of the *ton* wouldn't mind seeing a Windermere taken down a peg or two, let me tell you."

Though Valentina's palms had gone slick with sweat, Archie's smile remained cool and unbothered by Nestor's bluster. "I don't think you will."

"And why is that?"

Archie stuck two fingers into his mouth and let a piercing whistle fly. Near twenty men emerged from the stable, Papa in the middle. All the color drained from Nestor's face.

Archie nodded in the men's direction. "*They* are why."

"It's their word against mine," said Nestor with a bravado undermined by the bead of sweat that trickled down the side of his face.

"And it's your word against mine," said Archie, low and determined.

Valentina saw on Nestor's face the instant he realized not only wouldn't he get the horse, but he wouldn't be getting what he truly wanted, either.

His return to the top tier of Society.

That would be denied him forever.

The loss of the guineas would be nothing to that particular loss, which would sit like rot in his gut for the rest of his days.

Valentina felt not a shred of pity for the man.

This was justice served.

"Now, I'll tell you exactly what you're going to do," said

Archie. The chill and command in his voice sent a shiver slithering through Valentina. She wouldn't want to be on the receiving end of his ire. Just as he pursued pleasure relentlessly, so, too, did he pursue justice. He opened the trunk to reveal a cache of guineas. Five thousand pounds worth, to be exact. *"This* will be returned to its rightful owners, and *you* will leave England for one year."

"Leave England?" sputtered Nestor. "You must be as mad as they say. Where would I go?"

"Or would you rather stay and handle this matter in full view of Society?" Archie shrugged. "That option is also available to you. Makes no difference to me."

"You're serious," said Nestor.

"Utterly," said Archie.

Nestor's show of defiance fell entirely away, and he looked slightly winded. With a few words, his shadowy world built of envy, deceit, and lies had collapsed about his head. He gave his thigh three hard whacks with his palm, pivoted, and charged toward his coach-and-four.

"I'll give you three days to be out of London," Archie called to his back.

A cheer went up from Papa and his fellow tradesmen as Nestor's carriage rolled down the drive. For ten full minutes, Archie was the recipient of dozens of slaps to the back, while Valentina swiped more than a few tears from her eyes. These men—their livelihoods, their families—were saved.

And it was all because of the wild, mad, bold Viscount Archer.

They might not have a future together, but she would never regret their past.

He met her gaze over the crowd. How was it that so much could pass between them without words?

Leaving Papa and the other tradesmen to sort the money, he made his way toward her, stopping an awkward few feet away. Though short, that distance felt unbridgeable.

"Thank you," she said. Her stiff thanks felt wrong.

"I don't require gratitude from you, Valentina."

Her heart in her throat, she managed to nod. A question demanded oxygen. *And what do you require of me, Lord Archer?*

But she couldn't give it voice.

It was too intimate.

It would expose her fragile determination to move on with her life and create a fissure. From there, it would take very little— one of his smiles would do it—to crack that fissure wide open and have her all but begging for an *arrangement*.

Hoyden.

Papa joined them. "Valentina, it's time for us to leave. Your Mama will have worried her skirts to rags by now." He turned to Archie. "Would you join us for a meal, Lord Archer?"

"I'm afraid I have a previous engagement, Mr. Hart. So, I shall offer you my farewell here."

The men shook hands, and Valentina had to glance away. Archie, like her, understood this was the opportunity to break it off cleanly. Their lives apart had to begin sometime. They might as well start now.

When she dared turn, she found Archie facing her and extending his hand. "Miss Hart," he said, proper. "It was my pleasure."

Oh, those words in combination with a look in his eyes that only she knew weren't proper at all. After a moment's hesitation, she took his hand, though she knew she shouldn't touch him.

The handshake was over nearly as quickly as it had begun.

Yet her hand tingled with it, as she'd known it would.

Then she pivoted and was walking with Papa, a numbness in her body and mind.

That wasn't quite true.

Her right hand felt alive from his touch.

Oh, and one other feeling crawled through her.

Despair.

It felt wrong to leave Archie. And yet...

What choice had she?

Chapter Sixteen

A fortnight later

"**I**T'S THURSDAY," SAID Rory, clearly itching to remove himself from the tavern Archie had chosen for their night's carouse. "Don't you want to see what's happening at the Five Graces?"

Archie grunted into his beer. The dank and slightly murderous environs of The Toad's Hole suited his mood perfectly.

He'd only agreed to this night out with Rory because his friend was beginning his journey up to Scotland tomorrow. His father, the Earl of Carrick, had gifted his son with a Highland estate to run in preparation for his inevitable ascent to the earldom someday, and Rory had suddenly become quite serious about his lairding duties.

Rory consulted his gold pocket watch. "If we leg it right now, we could catch the chap with the monkey who—"

"*Not* the Five Graces," Archie all but growled. He hadn't been able to return to the Five Graces, not since *she* left.

In fact, he'd been keeping away from everything that reminded him of her. The Five Graces. His piano. Even his bed, choosing to sleep in a guest room. Everything that had once provided happiness, now only brought misery.

"You're gloomier than a Highland sky in January," groused Rory.

Again, Archie grunted. Of course, those other miseries were nothing to what he'd learned today. "She has a patron," he said.

"Who is it?"

It was telling that Rory didn't need to inquire as to the identity of *she*.

"Ravensworth." Archie could hardly get the name out of his mouth.

Rory's eyebrows drew together. "We're speaking of Miss Hart, correct?"

Archie gulped half his beer. "Aye," he said, swiping foam off his upper lip.

"He's patron to two opera singers now?" Rory shook his head, baffled. "Too much has never been enough for Ravensworth," he added with no small amount of admiration.

Archie had never before felt the compulsion to plant a facer on his good friend the Viscount Kilmuir, but the urge was itching in his right fist at this very moment. An urge he would resist. "Just the one that I've heard," he said.

Rory cocked his head. "Did Miss Hart change her name?"

"Possibly."

"To Fräulein Elsa Vogel?"

Now it was Archie's eyebrows drawing together. Valentina could hardly pull off the role of Italian contessa. A German fräulein? Doubtful.

Relief washed through him. "She didn't accept Ravensworth's patronage," he said, needing to speak the words aloud—needing them to be true.

Rory narrowed his gaze. People looked at Rory and saw little more than a hulking, handsome Scotsman who skimmed through life on the surfaces. But Rory possessed depths, and at this moment, his friend was peering at him from them. "Can I ask you a question, Archie?"

"Of course." He wouldn't like the question. He knew that much.

"What are you doing at The Toad's Hole with me?"

Archie held up his mug of beer. "Drinking to your safe journey."

Rory's eyebrows lifted in disbelief. That made two of them who knew Archie was lying. "Why aren't you with her?"

And there it was. The question he'd been avoiding asking himself this last fortnight. "I botched it," he said. It was only the truth.

"Seems to me you did a great service for her and her family."

"That's a separate matter."

Rory shrugged and shook his head. "What do I know about love, anyway? I wrote Miss Dalhousie quite the epic poem and still couldn't convince her to marry me." He clapped Archie on the back. "At least you tried."

In the spirit of honesty, Archie realized he needed to clear up a misconception. "I didn't ask Valentina to marry me."

Rory blinked. "You didn't?"

"I asked her... Well, I asked her..." He couldn't finish the sentence, aloud or in his mind.

"*Ah*," said Rory. "I don't know Miss Hart all that well, but even I could see she isn't the sort of lass who would accept an arrangement other than marriage."

The words slammed into Archie with the force of a typhoon, for they begged a question: How had he not seen it?

Valentina's words came to him.

Not even for you, Archie.

They'd been haunting him since she'd spoken them. But now, he saw something deeper than rejection nestled within them.

Longing.

It was there in that *even*.

And another fact hit him.

She would've said *yes* to the question he hadn't asked.

She wanted him. *Him.* The light and the dark. All of him.

And he wanted her. He wasn't sure he could create a life worth living without her, in truth.

So, it all begged yet another question—the most vital one...

If she wanted him, and he wanted her, then why on earth couldn't they have each other?

He shot to his feet. "Safe travels on your journey north, my friend, but I must go."

Rory stood and clapped Archie on the back. "I look forward to receiving a note bearing good news upon my arrival at Baile Ìm."

Then Archie was outside, boots clicking across filthy cobblestones at a clip almost as rapid as the race of his mind. He stuck two fingers in his mouth and hailed a hackney cab with a sharp whistle.

As he saw it, he had but one obstacle... How to win her?

But that was easy. He would win her with what had brought them together in the first place.

And he knew exactly how he would do it.

He had some labor ahead of him this night—of the manual variety.

VALENTINA SQUINCHED HER eyes shut against the music drifting through her dreams, trying to steal her away from slumber. She rolled onto her side and dragged a pillow over her head.

Through elusive sleep it hit her.

It wasn't just any music.

It was Archie's music.

And it wasn't coming from her dreams.

Her eyes flew open. Her room glowed a soft golden pink as dawn peeked through her curtains. The music was coming from beyond them. From...*outside*.

How was Archie's music coming from the high street?

Impossible.

Her pulse racing, she scrambled out of bed and darted to the window. Miss Hiss glared grumpily from her place on the bed, promising consequences for disturbing her sleep. Valentina would make it up to her later, but first she parted the curtain a sliver and peeked into the opening. She blinked once, then again.

There, in the middle of the high street, sat a piano.

Archie's piano.

With him seated on a bench before it, his fingers moving across the keyboard with expert ease, playing his music.

Their music—the music they'd made together.

Her heart forgot to beat for a few seconds.

A horse cart came within a few feet of the instrument. The farmer threw no few grouchy glances toward Archie as he maneuvered horse and cart around the piano and the strange aristocrat seated before it.

How had Archie managed to get the instrument there in the first place?

Valentina gave her head a tiny shake. He was Archie. That was how. Nothing was impossible for him. She loved that about him.

She startled backward, and the breath froze in her chest, her heart now a full gallop.

Loved?

She was afraid so.

A figure appeared in the open doorway. *"Colpo di fulmine,"* said Mama.

Valentina's eyebrows crinkled together. "What does that mean?"

"The thunderbolt," Mama clarified.

"The sky is quite clear this morning."

Mama laughed. "Not in the sky, *mia cara*. In *here*." She reached out and pressed the flat of her hand to the center of Valentina's chest. "Sometimes, love strikes here, so intense it cannot be denied." She nodded toward the window. "That is what he feels out there, and what you feel in *here*."

"What do I do, Mama?"

"He's met you half the distance. Now you must meet him the other half. That is how it's done in a marriage."

"Marriage?"

Oh, how to tell Mama it wasn't marriage that Archie wanted

from her?

And that her daughter might just be weak enough to accept less.

Mama nodded, a wise smile in her eyes. *"Si, mia cara."*

Valentina found that she was already halfway to the door when Mama said, "But, first, you must put this on." She was holding out a robe.

Valentina looked down to find she wore naught but her night chemise. Archie playing the piano in the middle of the Hampstead high street was shocking enough. But her joining him in nothing but a wisp of fabric would be one shock too many. The village might never recover.

She hastily donned the robe and all but flew down the corridor and stairs, not pausing to acknowledge the amused and questioning smirks from her brothers, who had gathered in their bedroom doorways. It was only when the front door bell jingled behind her, and her feet hit high street cobblestones, that her pace slowed. Actually, she ground to a complete stop, sudden shyness and uncertainty overcoming her as she watched Archie play, along with the small clusters of villagers who had gathered on their front doorsteps to watch this unexpected spectacle unfold. The passion Archie poured into the instrument beneath his fingertips, he drew out tenfold.

His clear blue gaze lifted and caught hers. Emotion and intensity shone out at her. So, too, did a smile. He was enjoying himself.

And she saw it.

His dark and light fused into a single whole.

He was playing for her, yes, but he was playing for an audience. He was revealing himself to the light.

For himself.

For her.

For *them*.

He was making an effort to be the man she'd always known he was.

He was meeting her more than halfway.

And now she must do the same.

She pushed off the door at her back and began to move toward him, unable not to for an instant longer, the magnetism between them too powerful to resist. She came to a stop in the bentside of the piano and rested her elbow on the fallboard, her gaze never once releasing his, as the vibrations of the music shook every cell in her body.

The final notes sounded and floated away on air bright with morning and the promise of a new day.

Not only that.

The promise of a new future.

But she didn't know how to make that first step forward. What to say to a man who made a gesture as grand as this? "Do you need something?" she asked.

A half smile curled along one side of his mouth, but his eyes remained serious. "Yes."

"What is that?" she asked, her mouth gone dry.

"*You.*"

"I thought we settled that." It had to be said.

He shook his head and stood. "A fortnight ago…"

"Yes?"

"I didn't ask you the correct question."

"Oh?" she asked on a rasped whisper—all the sound she was capable of making.

He rounded the piano and reached out, taking her hands in his. Warmth stole through her at the feel of his long, masculine fingers wrapped around hers.

"And what is the correct question?"

The other side of his mouth tipped into that irresistible smile of his. Whatever he was about to ask, she would say *yes* to. She wouldn't lose this man a second time. "Will you marry me?"

A collective gasp echoed around her. Valentina glanced around and noticed that more than half the village was watching the proceedings with bated breath.

For her part, Valentina hadn't gasped; her breath was caught somewhere in her throat.

Archie continued. "Because I'm a complete and utter dolt, it only occurred to me last night that you and I can have it all."

"And what is that?"

"Each other."

Valentina couldn't be certain, but she might've seen the grocer's wife swipe a tear away. Valentina felt more than a few of those welling in her eyes.

"All I want is you, Valentina. Your mind, your body"—the village gasped again—"your soul, if possible. I choose light. I choose *you* before this village, before all of England. Let's lead a life of our own creation, together."

Though his words were everything her heart wanted to hear, her pragmatic side reared its logical head. "You see my town. You've met my family. I wasn't raised to be the wife of a viscount."

"Oh, you'll be more than that someday. You'll be the wife of an earl."

"And what do I know about that?"

Why was she doing this? Why was she attempting to talk him out of his love for her?

His smile fell, and he became utterly serious. "Our life—the one we create, the one we live day by day, hour by hour, minute by minute—will have naught to do with a title. You keep my feet on the ground, Valentina. You let me fly."

And Valentina, at last, saw how it could work between them. "And you let me fly wild and free though my feet remain on the ground."

"You see? We are perfect for each other."

And she saw with perfect clarity that he was right.

"I'm utterly struck with love for you, Valentina."

"*Colpo di fulmine,*" she whispered.

"My Italian is a little rusty."

"The thunderstrike. *Here.*" She touched her chest. "And *here.*"

She touched the place directly above his heart.

Archie shook his head. "A thunderstrike is temporary. What exists between us is forever."

"Say *yes*, already," shouted a voice.

She smiled and no few tears broke and streamed down her cheeks. "Yes," she said. "Forever?" She had to hear it one more time.

He tucked his thumb beneath her chin and gently tugged her forward. *"Forever,"* he whispered into the scant space between their mouths, so only he and she could hear.

She trusted this man with her life, her body, her soul…her future. They completed each other in ways that only they knew.

"Kiss her already," came another shout. The voice sounded suspiciously like her little brother Luca.

"We can't keep our audience waiting," said Archie just before his mouth claimed hers.

Cheers and clapping sailed up to the sky. But Valentina had no care for them or the spectacle she and Archie were creating.

She would need to accustom herself to it, for life with this man who lit her soul—and thighs—on fire would never be boring or small or bound by society's rules.

Her arms wrapped around his neck, and she surrendered to his kiss, and to the life they would create together.

Epilogue

Florence
October 1823

ARCHIE WAS NERVOUS.

He wouldn't attempt to deny the fact as he sat in the fifth-row, crimson velvet theater seat, his hands clutched at his sides, his heart already a hammer in his chest.

The music hadn't even yet begun.

Not just any music.

His music.

A hand reached over, and elegant, feminine fingers twined through his. He wasn't alone, his wife's hand told him.

The theater was nearly full—a fact difficult to fathom. Theatergoers had come to hear his composition. It defied belief. Only two years ago, his work had never seen the light of day.

Of course, that was before Valentina had come along and altered the entire course of his life.

"So, what do you know about the Teatro della Pergola?" she asked, radiating with brightness. She ever led him out of his darkness, his wife.

"It was built in the seventeenth century by the Medici family," he said, glancing around the magnificent theater, all decked in crimson and gold.

"What didn't the Medicis have a hand in building in Florence?"

"Not much," he said on a laugh. He pointed his finger in the air and swooped it around. "The horseshoe shape with tiered family boxes to the sides? The first of its kind in Europe."

As Valentina took in the towering magnificence of the theater, Archie took her in. Somehow, in the two years since their marriage, her dark-eyed beauty had only grown more luminous as she'd settled into her roles of viscountess, wife, and muse, while retaining the parts of herself that made her Valentina—her pragmatism, her voice. That his muse had consented to share her life with him was the luckiest occurrence of his life.

The lights began to dim, and the theater settled into attention. It appeared to be a full house.

Valentina caught his gaze. He detected concern in those amber depths. "Are you ready?" she whispered.

"I suppose I don't have a choice," he said. He'd agreed to this concert, now he must see it through.

"You're a Windermere," she said, smiling. "You've always thrived by diving in head first."

Ah, his wife, she knew him well.

Yes, he was tetchy, but a case of nerves had never held him back from pursuing an interest once he'd taken it up. In fact, nerves only pushed and provoked him to new heights.

And his wife understood that about him.

She loved that about him.

The pianist, Signore Pasquini, strode to the center of the stage, dipped in a deep bow, and made his dignified way to the piano, flapping his coattails behind him as he lowered onto the bench. Signore Pasquini's fingers poised above the keyboard, anticipation roared through Archie's veins. In this silent moment before the music began not even a mote of dust dared stir.

Then Signore Pasquini's fingers depressed the keys, and *"Valentina by Night"* filled the theater.

To hear this piece played in the public sphere filled a space inside Archie he'd never known existed. It made him feel whole and complete, and somehow, strangely, useful.

Which wouldn't have been possible without the woman sitting beside him.

Moreover, none of it would possess meaning without her.

The piece reached its end with a flourish of climax. Archie could appreciate that Signore Pasquini was quite the masterful pianist. The next instant, the crowd broke into wild applause, and something cracked open inside Archie. *Pride...relief.*

He turned toward Valentina, for it was only her appreciation that truly mattered.

If she deemed his work—*him*—worthy, then it—and he—were.

"You moved them, Archie," she said. "This is all for you."

Archie shook his head. "And *you*, my love." Unable not to, he reached out and cupped the back of her head. "I'm only good for a lark and a laugh without you, my wild Valentina. I can only imagine what new adventures await us."

"You won't have to imagine for long," she said. He only now noticed the secret smile curving her lush ruby-red lips.

"How do you mean?"

She took his hand and placed it low on her stomach. "I'd say you'll only have to imagine for about seven months."

Sudden joy surged through him. "Do you mean..."

She nodded, happy tears sparkling in her eyes.

The wild "Whoop!" that Archie let rip drew no fewer than half the eyes in the theater. No matter. There was simply no containing it.

Let the world see his happiness.

Let the world see his love.

"You've given me the best night of my life," he said, drawing her close. "And what have I given you?"

She didn't hesitate. "The ability to fly. This life of laughter and *us*."

"Shall we retire to the villa and see how much better we can make this night?" He waggled his eyebrows, so there was no mistaking his meaning.

"You are incorrigible, husband," she said, shaking her head. "We must wait until after everyone has showered you with rightful praise."

"You drive a hard bargain, wife."

"Isn't that what you love about me?"

"Amongst other parts of you." He flashed her the wicked smile that he knew melted her to the core.

"I believe you'll have to settle for a kiss for now."

Oh, didn't his wife know him at all?

If his wife wanted a kiss, he would give it to her.

And if she was expecting a chaste kiss…

Nay, she wouldn't be expecting a chaste kiss.

She knew her husband.

His mouth claimed hers with all the passion and fire that hadn't cooled a degree from the first time he'd kissed her two years ago.

And when he finally released her from the kiss, both of them slightly panting, she would know that he intended to make good on his promise of what would come later.

And for the rest of their days.

The End

About the Author

Sofie Darling is an award-winning author of historical romance. The third book in her Shadows and Silk series, Her Midnight Sin, won the 2020 RONE award for Best Historical Regency.

She spent much of her twenties raising two boys and reading every romance she could get her hands on. Once she realized she simply had to write the books she loved, she finished her English degree and embarked on her writing career. Mr. Darling and the boys gave her their wholehearted blessing.

When she's not writing heroes who make her swoon, she runs a marathon in a different state every year, visits crumbling medieval castles whenever she gets a chance, and enjoys a slightly codependent relationship with her beagle, Bosco.

CPSIA information can be obtained
at www.ICGtesting.com
Printed in the USA
LVHW081746070922
727717LV00010B/203

9 781958 098554